Near a Wild & Dark Shore

Damien Scott

Willingness

In Part I, a typology of five discourses about womanhood that are common in unusual cases of women killing is developed: the attractive woman; the conflict between virtuosity and fantasy; the one who has been hurt;

The powerful lady; the witch as well. It outlines the components of each discourse and investigates how they emerged by reviewing well-known examples. Part I argues that these depictions may reveal significant moments and anxieties associated with social change.

A shift to a more unambiguous setting, which was the subject of the exploratory evaluation drove for this book, is the mark of combination of Part II, which is disconnected into three sections. The typology of surprising cases, including ladies what kill's identity is, utilized in an examination of the case reports of 12 ladies who were blamed for crime in England and Grains somewhere in the range of 1957 and 1966. This is portrayed as an important period in English history in Section 1. It inspects the connection between direction ideas and the significant social and social developments of the time. In addition, it acknowledges the significance of war-related advancement expectations and anxieties. Additionally, this chapter addresses the methodological issues associated with archival and documentary research and provides an overview of the discourse analysis methods used in the analysis. The five discourses on womanhood and the 12 women who have been accused of shocking murders are examined in Section 2. The 12 cases are analyzed to decide how they connect with the moving social and social limits of the time as well as what they say regarding the norms of gentility that are common in the current day. Each talk takes place in Britain and Ridges during the twentieth century. The issues that arise from these cases in terms of orientation guidelines and the social repercussions of homicide are brought together toward the end of Section 3.

The masculine lady The portrayal of fierce way of behaving as masculine has brought about irregular decreases in the quantity of female killers. This portrayal recommends that awful women are more like men than women and are not really women using any and all means. There are numerous explanations for female criminal behavior that point to manifestations of female masculinity, and the criminological paradigm of the masculine criminal woman is deeply ingrained. This section will provide additional information on these. This tendency to masculinize characters is made worse when women are perceived as lesbians. Lesbianism and manliness have generally been connected by criminological speculations about the association between elevated manliness in ladies and the affinity to affront and natural and mental clarifications of ladies' homosexuality.

This section looks at how cases where women are blamed for shocking homicides show the manly woman talk. The various interpretations of the term "female masculinity" as a pathological construct will first be examined. After that, it investigates the well-known cases of Rose West, Aileen Wuornos, and Wanda Jean Allen to determine the origin of this discussion.

The manly woman of criminal science In positivist criminal science, the connection between criminal women and manliness first emerged. In Lombroso's groundbreaking Criminal Woman, which was first published in Italy in 1885, the embodied masculine characteristics of female criminals were identified. As indicated by Lombroso, ladies were dull and conventionalist essentially, so they were not organically inclined toward overstep the law. This did not imply that women had superior morality; rather, their aloof demeanor was the reason for their congruence. Lombroso argued that "normal" women appeared more masculine and had fewer physical flaws and abnormalities. Before his work on ladies, his comparably organically determined speculations of male criminal way of behaving were undermined (Crossbeam and Gibson, 2004). This was primarily because there had not been enough studies done on women's criminal behavior. Notwithstanding the way that standard criminal science had dismissed the possibility that genuine flaw showed culpability by the center of the twentieth 100 years, Criminal Woman, which was converted into English in 1903 and became known as The Female Liable party, was the main huge criminological text on female culpability.

The alleged link between masculine women and criminality was further developed by criminologists in the twentieth century.

According to Glueck and Glueck (1934), women with masculine bodies were more likely to commit crimes and could choose an aggravating behavior. Cowie and others 1968) focused in on delinquent young women and fought that particular genuine qualities, for example, being colossal, will undoubtedly make young women savage. Young female offenders were naturally more masculine. These studies, in contrast to Lombroso's, did not suggest that a specific physical stigmata predicted criminal behavior. But they kept spreading the myth that women who were truly manly would always break the law.

Other theories have proposed a link between women's masculinity and criminal behavior, in addition to biological explanations for female criminal behavior. Different scholars fight that ladies' mental dismissal of womanliness or recognizable proof with manliness is an indicator of criminal way of behaving.

Thomas (1923) recommended that ladies who need to have some good times and be enthusiastic could pass on their tiresome responsibilities to search for open doors and experience. Criminologists have also argued, utilizing Freudian concepts regarding the identification of gender roles, that women who do not develop normal feminine attitudes run the risk of becoming delinquent (Klein, 1973; Widom, 1979).

Finally, humanistic explanations for why women could commit dreadful approach to acting have in like manner proposed that women who execute 'dynamic' or frustrated

dreadful approaches to acting hold masculine characteristics. This dispute was started by Parsons (1947), who argued that young men's defiance can be seen as an effort to distance themselves from their mothers and spread out their masculinity. However, young women are expected to follow the example set by their mothers and obey the law. Cohen adopted a portion of Parsons' proposal in his 1955 study of bad behavior among young men. Criminal activity may "verify" a boy's masculinity for working-class boys, which may be hindered by their limited opportunities. Because of the assumption that they would keep away from crime to become ladies, young ladies were presumably going to be conformist. Sexual indiscrimination was the consequence of young ladies' uprisings as opposed to demonstrations of viciousness or guiltiness. They had been looking for a female accomplice up until this point.

According to Whitehead (2005), these sociological studies established a strong connection between criminology and criminal behavior as a means of expressing or achieving masculinity. Byrne and Trew, 2008). According to Parsons and Cohen, the masculine gender role is associated with women who commit masculine crimes like murder. The ideal way to end this is this.

Some criminological studies on women in prison, according to Widom (1979), examined their value systems to determine whether they held masculine or feminine values. The idea that women's guilt is typically in line with their femininity has emerged as a result of theories about orientation and job socialization. Women, for example, might shoplift in order to get food or other necessities for their families. When men commit the heinous act of taking goods, women frequently act as their accomplices. As per ladies' lobbyist and wrongdoing expert Naffine (1985, 1987), the direction work socialization proposition is precarious on the grounds that it reifies masculinity and womanliness, expecting these ideas can be typically portrayed and assessed. Additionally, it overlooks significant variations in individuals' social control, which may influence their culpable behavior.

In the end, these criminological hypotheses about how manliness, gentility, and wrongdoing are linked portray women who commit brutal crimes as crazy and crazy-minded. Bombed ladies are women who engage in particular types of misconduct because they project a manly image. This is true regardless of whether it is due to their tendency to be more like men, intellectual hurt, or a connection with "some unacceptable" direction.

Klein (1973) claims that feminist criminologists have refuted the notion that women who commit particular types of crimes are masculine and have questioned negative and stereotypical perceptions of criminal women. Naffine in 1987; Daly, 1997; 2006, Lind-Chesney). Despite this, due to its widespread acceptance, it is essential to investigate the legacy of the masculine woman in criminology. Recent research (Chesney-Lind and Eliason, 2006) on depictions of violence against girls have shed light on the emergence of discourses concerning masculinization in relation to girls who are involved in gang violence. 2006) Ringrose In popular representations of crime, such as news sources, films, television shows, and true crime, the "masculine woman" discourse is articulated as an explanation for women's violence or killing. According to Beam (2007), it is essential to take such "well-known criminal science" seriously because it is the primary means by which the majority of people learn about wrongdoing.

In sexology, another intellectual field that has produced discourses of the masculine woman, the scientific study of sex has produced discourses of the masculine woman. In the late nineteenth century, authors like Krafft-Ebing (1894) and Ellis (1897) attempted to list, group, and comprehend various sexual personalities. Sexology began in this way. Sexologists in the nineteenth century zeroed in on homosexuality in all kinds of people, characterizing it as sexual reversal. Male gay individuals were made sure to have a great deal of qualities that were female, while female gay individuals were made sure to have a ton of attributes that were male.

Reversal was seen as an organic birth deformity by sexologists in the nineteenth hundred years. According to Foucault (1990), the body may be the key to understanding homosexuality. Vicinus; 1992; Bland, 2002).

By arguing that there were four distinct types of lesbians, each more manly and ruffian than the others, Krafft-Ebing made the first logical attempt to organize female homosexuality in 1894. As indicated by Krafft-Ebing, the fourth classification, the rearrange, "has of the female characteristics just the genital organs:

Refered to in Newton, 1994, p. 566: " Everything the man thinks, feels, does, and even looks like is his. Lesbianism remembered dressing for drag and excusing traditional social positions, despite how Krafft-Ebing was made as a characteristic condition. Also, as opposed to sexual way of behaving, he underlined attributes and qualities.

Other sexologists agreed that lesbianism should be seen as

inversion. According to Ellis (1897), homosexuality is an acquired trait that cannot be changed. According to Hirschfeld (1913), sexual disturbances are of the third sex and depict people of one sex trapped in the body of another. In the late nineteenth and mid 20th hundreds of years, European sexologists contended that transforms should be given privileges and approached with deference. Their work was completed to determine human sexuality, not to disparage gay people (Magee and Mill operator, 1992; Bland, 2002). Notwithstanding this, how gay bodies were depicted as "blemished" and "savage" laid out a structure for considering lesbianism bizarre and eventually disturbing (Foucault, 1990).

The scenario of a "manly" woman who committed murder energized the development of the female reverse idea in sexology. In the first American edition of Sexual Reversal, which was published in 1901 (Duggan, 1993, p. 795) Alice Mitchell, a 19-year-old woman who cut Freda Ward's jugular in Memphis, Tennessee, in 1892, was portrayed by Ellis as a "normal alteration." Alice had made a number of proposals to be engaged to her extremely dear companion Freda. When it appeared that she no longer loved Freda, Alice made the decision to kill her rather than break up with her. The case stood out enough to be noticed from the media, which considered it an "unnatural bad behavior." Alice's lawyers underscored her manly way of behaving and indifference for female pursuits like sewing and embroidery as a component of a madness guard (Duggan, 1993; in 1995 by Lindquist). Sexuality historians have examined the significance of her case as a prominent construction of the new lesbian subjectivity of the late nineteenth century (Duggan, 1993; 1995 Lindquist; According to Waters (1999), later psychoanalytic understandings of sexuality emphasized sexuality's psychological importance over its natural etiology. The Freudian concept of hetero womanliness and masculinity as signs of improvement influenced the mid-twentieth century perspective on homosexuality as a mental disorder (Weeks, 1985). Jennings asserts that in the 1950s and 1960s, the majority of scientific definitions and classifications of sexuality were psychiatric. Diverse hypotheses showed that lesbian women were thought to be young, ugly, and at risk of displaying masculine traits (Magee and Plant administrator, 1992; Hart, 1994; Jennings, 2004).

According to Conrad and Angell (2004), therapy discovered that heterosexuality was linked to excellent psychological health. As a result, some mental health professionals held the belief that homosexuality was a sign of mental illness or a mental maladjustment that could not be helped by anyone else. According to Karpman (1951), writing about crackpots in the early and middle of the 20th century suggested a link between psychopathy and sexual deviation, which included homosexuality. Crazy person, psychopathy, and psychopathic person all have different general implications. But McCord and McCord (1964) say that a "psychopath" is someone who doesn't have a moral compass, a conscience, or the ability to build relationships that last a lifetime. Freedman (1987) says that in the middle of the 20th century, the term "sexual psychopath" was especially popular in the United States.

According to Shotwell, 1946, refered to in Freedman, 1996, p. 405, mental assessments coordinated in the US during the 1940s, "the possibly more important penchant of the [female] neurotic to partake in sex acts with various young women" proposed a relationship among psychopathy and lesbianism. In the Bound Together Domain and the United States, female-only groundworks began to be viewed with uncertainty as favorable locations for gay activity between women. According to Jennings, this included concerns regarding boarding schools, all-women's colleges, and prisons.

It is essential to acknowledge that not all sexology views lesbianism as pathological. Near sex encounters ought to be seen as normal, as shown by the Kinsey expounds on American sexual approach to acting from 1948 and 1953. According to Taylor (1999), their prevalence suggested that heterosexuality's dominance was largely attributable to social norms. Other studies from the middle of the 20th century suggested that homosexuality, a biological trait shared by humans and monkeys, existed. The purpose of this section, on the other hand, is to trace the cycles of the manly woman's speech and to demonstrate the presence of the manly woman in bizarre instances of women who kill, where pathology has frequently been mentioned.

Starting in the last part of the 1960s, activists who were lesbian, gay, and women's activist tested the possibility that lesbianism implied anomaly, deviation, and pathology (Cruikshank, 1992; Weeks (2007) (Jones, 2007a) claims that abnormality is no longer the most common discourse construct of lesbian identity. The American Mental Affiliation remembered homosexuality for its rundown of mental problems in 1973. Nevertheless, the World Wellbeing Association did not officially recognize homosexuality as a mental illness until 1988. As indicated by Taylor (1999), homosexuality was likewise eliminated from the English Definite and Authentic Manual of Mental Issues (DSM) during this time. This exhibits that ace clinical gatherings kept on involving homosexuality as a sickness model after the center of the twentieth hundred years. Furthermore, it is crucial for remember that, very much like the manly lady of criminal science, outdated thoughts of lesbian personality that connect it to viciousness and wrongdoing keep on being a piece of well known criminal science, which can be found in news stories, films, network shows, and genuine wrongdoing. They are still present, according to Thomas, in legal constructions of lesbian subjectivity.

Negative and derogatory depictions of female masculinity have dominated understandings of putatively masculine criminal women, according to Heidensohn (1996). This does not imply the absence of particular depictions of female masculinity. For instance, according to Duggan (1993), the subjectivity that women of the early twentieth century were promised would be the "mannish lesbian" stereotype. This generalization was made when sexologists built the upset in the nineteenth 100 years. Whimsical researcher Newton Halberstam (1998) fights that masculine female subjectivities can be given power and pride. In any case, well-known or legitimate depictions of women who kill rarely feature these liberating conversations and subjectivities.

The spasmodic appearance of the manly woman as a freak communicating for the vast majority of communicating express friendly strains associating with critical quality and right way to deal with acting is one factor that contributes to the lack of additional freeing talks and subjectivities. As was referenced before, these worries are especially centered around culture as a picture of social limits. The assumed masculinity of women, particularly in relation to violence, is frequently portrayed in conservative discourses as a worrying power grab and a sign of cultural decline.

Moving orientation and sexual relationship standards frequently coincide with this. Three surprising instances of female homicide in the latter part of the 20th century that were influenced by manly lady talk are the focus of this section.

Heather, Rose West's 16-year-old natural daughter, was considered to be legitimately responsible for the murders of ten young women and girls in Britain in 1995. Their bodies were found in the nursery and storm cellar of the Gloucester home that she and her better half Fred shared. Additionally, Fred was held accountable for the murders, but he took his own life while awaiting preliminary hearings (Cameron, 1996; Exactly when Rose appeared in court in the winters of 2002 and 2004, she was

41 years old, married, and a mother. Rose gained the typically masculine moniker "chronic executioner" as a result of the numerous casualties.

She was found guilty of the murders over the course of twenty years. Casualties experienced physical and sexual maltreatment. The arraignment's case and Rose's conviction were significantly impacted by the sexual abnormality and alleged manliness of the evidence presented at her initial. She denied contributing, there was no legal evidence to link her to the murders, and Fred promised that he would be solely responsible for their bonus before he passed away. According to Winter (2002, 2004), practically identical truth verification is when evidence is provided to support a person's commitment to activities comparable to those for which they are targeted. As a result, the conflict surrounding the arraignment relied on similar truth confirmation. Three female survivors at Rose West's start said that she attacked them and really handled them in the same way the casualties were treated. Rose was seen as at real fault for crime based on this statement.

Details of Rose's masculine-type sexual violence, such as using a vibrator to commit sexual assault, were included in the surviving women's testimony (Winter, 2002). Fred was depicted as a latent spectator while she was depicted as the assailant in these assaults. despite the fact that Fred's daughter and Rose's stepdaughter, one of the observers, had been abused multiple times as a child. Rose was made to appear to be a physically dominant, assertive man, which made her more masculine and brought attention to her sexual inclinations. In addition, it demonstrated how far she went against the ideal of femininity and motherhood. The prosecution successfully mobilized the masculine woman discourse during Rose West's trial to support her conviction (Winter, 2004). This demonstrates that the significance of this discourse extends beyond just the formation of deviant subjectivities; Additionally, it might have an impact on the decision or, possibly, the punishment imposed on the woman who is being referred to.

It was extremely surprising when the West defense claimed that Rose was involved in what could frequently be considered extremely masculinized sequential killings. However, everyday sociocultural shifts in England in the 1990s also contributed to the emergence of the manly lady talk. According to Wykes (1998), the Wests were a typical heterosexual family. This kind of family started to lose its power during the 1990s as the affirmation of single-parent families extended and marriage ended up being less significantly a need. Rodger (1995) says that the Moderate Government's questionable "straightforward" crusade, which focused "conventional" values like the holiness of the family unit, was extremely moralistic in its reaction to these changes, which not every person upheld.

From that point forward, this mission has been portrayed as a representation of the Moderate government's failure to appreciate the moving moral scene in England during the 1990s (Weeks, 2007; Quinn, 2008). Rose West, a married mother who was charged with murder and sexual assault, proved to moderates that the "standard" family is widespread. As a result, she was open to being portrayed as a vengeful "stranger" who should have been disowned in order to restore the ideal of the nuclear family (Bauman, 1991).

The following section examines two examples of masculine and feminine discourse articulation: American ladies Wanda Jean

Allen and Aileen Wuornos In both their preliminaries and media inclusion of their cases, they were depicted as physically degenerate and manly. In 2001 and 2002, Aileen and Wanda were both executed in isolated states. In the United States, gender and the death penalty scholars assert that lesbian women are underrepresented on death row. Female respondents appear to be dehumanized by a crucial method for obtaining a woman's capital conviction (Farr, 1999;

2002, Streib; Head honcho, 2005).1 The meaning of these ladies' entwined personalities is accentuated specifically. In spite of the way that this was in no way, shape or form the main strategy by which these cases were built, the cases are analyzed as per the conversation of masculine women. Feminist academics and commentators have supported Miller Aileen's claim that she killed her victims in self-defense (Chesler, 1993; Working on behalf of the two women and highlighting legal issues with their convictions, groups for common liberties and against the death penalty, 2004). Hart, 1994), and emphasize the significance of her abuse experiences as a child and as an adult. Notwithstanding, the otherworldly social portrayal of these two cases has been the conversation of the manly lady. Additionally, it had a significant impact on the challenges faced by both women.

Aileen Wuornos's case is well-known. She was the focus of the huge Hollywood movie Beast; Aileen has been the subject of two full length narratives: Aileen's 1992 book, The Selling of a Constant Executor: Life and Death of a Constant Killer (2003), in addition to two films that were made for television in any case. Numerous news articles and fictional depictions of actual crimes have also been written about her case. This fascination is fueled by her extremely unusual murders and the dubious FBI definition of her as "America's first female serial killer" (Kohn, 2001; 2007 Pearson). According to Arrigo and Williams (2006), the numerous depictions have nearly rendered Aileen's situation hyperreal. It is challenging to recover the "legitimate" Aileen from this abundance of frequently defamatory images; regardless, a women's lobbyist interpreting these photos can challenge them (Naffine, 1997).

When Aileen Wuornos was put to death in Florida in 2002, she was 46 years old.

She was found guilty in 1991 of the murders of seven men between the years 1988 and 1989. She met the men she killed on the grounds that she made her living as a prostitute2. Along the interstate roadway, Aileen moved toward clients, periodically pretending pain to allure men to stop.

She shot and killed her victims after convincing or coercing them to remove their clothing. Also, it was thought that she killed them and took their money. Exactly when the men ended up being undesirable and endeavored to go after her, Aileen made it clear right from the outset that she had killed them genuinely. She later withdrew this statement, claiming it was fabricated and reserved the right to seek the death penalty (Hart, 1994; Miller at the time; 2007 Pearson). Shipley and Arrigo (2004) say that even though psychiatric evaluations showed that Aileen had serious emotional and mental health issues, she was still considered competent to be executed and didn't get any help for her mental health while she was on death row.

It is fundamental to understand the social, social, and financial meaning of the parts of Aileen Wuornos' personality to examine the development of her way of life as a manly lady. Aileen came from an unfortunate family in Michigan. Despite the fact that she and her sibling were taught as children that they belonged to their parents, Aileen was raised by her grandparents. Additionally, their mother had left the house when they were young, and their father was never a part of their lives. At the point when Aileen was 15 years of age, her granddad physically manhandled her, and she brought forth a kid that might have been his. The child was wanted for adoption. She occasionally rested harshly in the forest as a young adult, and meetings with her media companions reveal that she was seriously dismissed and abused. Aileen worked as a prostitute from her mid-teenage years until her arrest and imprisonment in 1991, when she was 35 (Griggers, 1995; Williams and Arrigo, 2006) At the time of the murders and up until her arrest, Aileen was dating Tyria Moore. In exchange for avoiding arraignment as a co-conspirator, Tyria provided evidence against her (Hart, 1994;

(2004) Mill operator Aileen Wuornos was portrayed in the media as a "Deadly Lesbian Whore" and a "Bull-Dyke Alpha predator" due to her lesbian sexual orientation (Farr, 1999, p. 60). The way that Aileen was a wild lady who was likewise having a sexual relationship with one more lady was faulted for her aggression. This was the case because Aileen was a "manly lesbian." According to Hart (1994), her subversion of the typical violence that occurs between male clients and female prostitutes, in which the client rapes or assaults the woman, was viewed as additional evidence of her masculinity.

More details about the murders made Aileen's image of herself as a macho woman even worse. Since she met her victims while requesting on the road, her behavior has been portrayed as "savage" (Silvio et al., 2006). It was portrayed as a deceptive display of womanliness that was intended to deceive male drivers in court and in the media. Her attempt to portray pain or trouble in order to get men to stop their cars was unsuccessful. Instead of being a genuine "damsel in distress," Aileen was a masculinized serial killer (Pearson, 2007). In any event, when she killed a lady, she defied the guidelines. She killed outside in the open street and masculine space, not inside a house. She was therefore especially unsettling. In addition to disrupting the socially accepted practice of including violence in paid sex, she adopted a "manly" method of finding and killing victims, earning her the title of "first female chronic executioner" (Warf and Waddell, 2002;

2007 Pearson).

The intersection of Aileen's gender and sexuality is the most obvious illustration of how aspects of her identity were constructed through the discourse of the masculine woman. The portrayal of her as aggressive and masculine emphasized her sexual deviance and lesbianism a lot. Regardless, the masculine woman talk moreover used various pieces of her character. For adequate womanliness, white working-class gentility is the standard. Aileen had been a member of a social class that was lower than her own. She had perpetually been poor, and she made her living by taking, filling in as a prostitute, and theft. She was seen as uncouth and, as a result, masculine just by being there;

She was accused of violating notions of feminine decorum by yelling and swearing during her trial, according to Basilio (1996).

As a white woman from a poor, unstable country establishment who had led a migrant and criminal presence, Aileen was at the bottom of the white social request (Griggers, 1995). In the United States, social class and "race" or personality are typically intertwined. As per Wray (2006), she was viewed as "white rubbish," a term that alludes to inbreeding, viciousness, and an absence of schooling. According to Griggers (1995), her social personality was one of shame rather than authenticity. Wray (2006) shows that people who are called "white garbage" stay away from the boundaries of whiteness. They are "not precisely white" in view of their despicable characters. Aileen's reputation as "white waste" grew as a result of the manly woman talk, as the "trash" label is both degrading and a sign of vanity. Despite the fact that Aileen Wuornos was primarily portrayed as "different" and "abnormal" due to crossing the boundaries of femininity and heterosexuality, Griggers (1995) stated that her poverty, lack of family, and status as a prostitute were the primary distinctions that set her apart from middle-class Americans.

Consider the combination of social and social factors that led to Aileen's 1991 conviction. Chesney-Lind (2006) emphasized how the negative portrayal of Aileen Wuornos contributed to a "backlash" against feminism and the broader emancipation of women. Faludi is the source of the concept of "backfire," which describes the rise of anti-women activist speech and policymaking in the United States in the 1980s. According to page 14, "set off by the expanded chance that they could win it, rather than by ladies' accomplishment of full equity," this was the situation. By the beginning of the 1990s, the lesbian and gay liberation movement in the United States had also made significant, but contested, progress (Cruikshank, 1992). Aileen was worked as a "man pundit" as a part of the moderate response to these social changes (Robson, 1997) and as a picture of the dangers of lady's privileges and lesbian opportunity.

Aileen Wuornos's case is more well-known all over the world than Wanda Jean Allen's. However, her execution in Oklahoma in 2001 was extensively covered by the American media (Shipman, 2002). In 1988, she fought with her partner Gloria Leathers outside a police station and killed her. Wanda had as of late shot and killed a woman twice. After she killed her girlfriend Dedra Pettus in 1981 during a dispute, she was found guilty of manslaughter. Gloria was avowed to have been shot by Wanda out of fear that Gloria would head out in different directions from her.

Then again, Wanda said that Gloria scared her and made her fear for her life. Gloria had previously murdered a partner, and Wanda and Gloria met while both were in prison (Baker, 2008; 2008, Philofsky).

The prosecution claimed that Wanda was the more dominant member of the relationship, despite the fact that it appears that the two women engaged in acts of violence toward one another. The day Gloria was shot by Wanda, Gloria struck her with a garden rake, injuring her face (Shortnacy, 2001; Mogul, 2005). Due to the fact that Wanda was in a car accident when she was 12 and suffered brain damage, the defense argued that she had a learning disability. Wanda was also stabbed in the head when she was a teenager. Despite having an IQ of 69, which falls within the range of what is considered to be low functioning, the state of Oklahoma executed her (Baker, 2008). Because no evidence of her insufficiency was presented during the special starter, this avoidance was looked for and used as the basis for the offer (Streib, 2002).

African American lesbian Wanda She truly centered around her more energetic kinfolk as a youth in a sad family with only one parent. She was captured on numerous occasions when she was a high schooler for taking food and dress for her kin. Her mother was also an alcoholic and had learning disabilities. As indicated by Bread Cook (2008), the assurance of government help empowered Wanda and Gloria to live as grown-ups. A conflict with respect to an organization help rotate toward the sky while looking for food lighted their contention on the day Gloria was shot (Investor, 2005).

During Wanda's preliminary, the manly lady talk was expressly used to build her. The prosecution referred to her as "manly" and the "man" of her relationship with Gloria, according to Shortnacy (2001). Mogul, 2005). Cook (2008) likewise expressed that Wanda "wore the pants." p. 80). Through the persistent "switch" talk, this portrayal clearly relied on a negative and homophobic development of Wanda's sexuality. In her first, her sexual orientation was used as a legally disturbing factor, with sexological claims about the pathology and deviation of lesbian connections being repeated.

Examining the associations that exist between Wanda's "race," orientation, and sexuality to fathom the event of the manly lady talk in her case is essential. In social settings, African-American and lesbian women have a long history of being referred to as "manly." Farr asserts that African-American women who identify as lesbians are more likely to be viewed as masculine. The initial arraignment of Wanda utilized stereotypes of the "dark beast" as well as the forceful, macho lesbian (Alford,

2006). Seitz (2005) says that this development underlines the savageness, risk, and inborn culpability of African-American respondents. The jury was given a gorilla-themed card in the indictment with the clever inscription "Persistence my ass, I will kill something." The lawyer expressed, "That is Wanda Jean Allen basically," contrasting the African American lady with a gorilla (Alford, 2006, page 342). Lombroso's "atavistic" anthropological criminology, which compared the criminal body to apes, is comparable to this strategy. According to Seitz (2005), it also implies well-established racist beliefs that African Americans are sexually immoral and crude. Magnate (2005) claims that Wanda was denied an appeal due to her preliminary's homophobic and bigoted explanations. Wanda was therefore unable to overturn her execution.

Philofsky (2008) asserts that Wanda's socioeconomic status had a significant impact on the masculine woman discourse. In the US and different nations, social class and "race" are built through communication, as was examined comparable to Aileen Wuornos. Gloria and Wanda were regarded as members of the "underclass" due to their dependence on government assistance, and Wanda's unfortunate family ancestry would have exacerbated this perception. The urban underclass, which gained prominence in the 1980s in the United States, was defined by theorists like Murray. He argued that welfarist policies of the 1960s undermined family and individual responsibility and created a subclass that was dependent and obsessed.

Murray made single-parent families and other issues like learning disabilities and alcoholism a special part of this social event.

As per Simon (1993), specialists on the chance of the underclass have brought up that its improvement in the US is racialized and habitually utilized as disparaging truncation for the metropolitan African-American populace.

Because of the perception that she was not only dangerous and sexually deviant but also a member of the underclass, Wanda was further defeminized and portrayed as a masculine woman. Wanda's identification with the urban poor emphasized her distance from conventional femininity.

Like Aileen, Wanda's alleged "abnormality" was brought on by her sexual orientation and being excluded from middle-class life's luxuries.

Aileen and Wanda can be understood as the bearers of shameful identities that served as a representation of the violence of being marginalized.

During the 1980s, African-American ladies' detainment rates soar because of negative depictions of them as crooks, especially corresponding to the deal and utilization of rocks (Maher, 1992; (This was made possible in the United States by policies that moved away from welfare-based approaches to criminal justice and were "tough on crime" (Pasko and Chesney-Lind, 2004).

Simon, 2007). Despite the fact that Wanda Jean's case had nothing to do with drug use, at a time when African American women were frequently depicted as criminals and a threat to society, she was held accountable.

While endeavoring to grasp the improvement of conversations with respect to bizarre ladies who kill, the occurrences of Aileen Wuornos and Wanda Jean Allen exhibit the meaning of utilizing a technique that incorporates various features. In the two occasions, the manly lady talk relied fairly upon profoundly grounded connection between manliness, hostility, and lesbianism. However, it also relied on social representations of "race" and "class," which emphasize poor women and those whose racial characteristics are excluded from the feminine ideal. Aileen and Wanda were finally made to appear to have virtually no moral worth as a result of this conversation, which may have made their executions more agreeable (Farr, 1999). Despite the fact that Aileen Wuornos and Wanda Jean Allen had learning disabilities and issues with their emotional well-being, they were still executed because of the strength of this desultory development.

Taking into account the meaning of the characters' game plan of the two ladies' intersection and its effect on their cases. Aileen and Wanda, both horrible women, relied on court-appointed public defenders, who have a terrible track record protecting capital cases in the United States. Cook (2008) asserts that Wanda's attorney had never tried a capital case before and had not presented evidence of her learning disabilities at her initial hearing. As per Broomfield (2003), Aileen's attorney, who went by the name "Dr Legitimate," showed up in court while high and encouraged her to argue "no challenge" to five of the homicides for which she was sentenced, in spite of the way that this didn't diminish the sentence she got. According to O'Shea (1999, p. 21), public safeguards typically need to be very junior, have some expertise in other areas like separation suits, or have experience managing the complexities of capital cases. Public shields serve over 90% of those anticipating execution in the US.

Master developments of female manliness in sexology and criminal science shaped the manly lady conversation. An examination of three instances of strange homicide committed by ladies in the late 20th century uncovers that the atypical manly lady torment social and legitimate developments 100 years after the fact, regardless of the way that these developments from the nineteenth century are never again part of most of standard scholastic talk.

In addition to breaking the rules of propriety, masculine women who kill also use violence to make themselves appear to be men, which makes them disturbing figures. The fact that criminal women are portrayed as men is based on reality and has been demonstrated repeatedly. Especially, the cases show the way that moderate conversations can include the masculine woman in light of moving sexual direction and connections, especially as mistreated sexual directions and characters like womanhood and lesbianism gain power.

The dream or genius divide exists when female accomplices kill someone else. The polarity of the dream or driving force exists. Either as collaborators who are profoundly influenced by their partners or lovers or as domineering, manipulative women who can get men to do what they want is how these women can be portrayed. In these instances, the woman in question is frequently depicted in both constructions, making her ultimately inaccessible. There can be a lot of vulnerability, but she either controls her male partner or is in love with him, depending on which portrayal is "right." This suggests that it is difficult to determine the lady's level of involvement in the wrongdoing or violations, which raises questions about her true essence. The nature of femininity is the subject of debate on both sides of the dichotomy in accordance with heterosexuality guidelines. Stresses over women being related with murders with men are reflected in greater social issues in view of the area and time of the killings4. Despite the fact that it is essential to acknowledge that these standards are fluid and change over time and across societies, it is possible to speculate about the heteronormative origins of womanliness. These beliefs suggest that manliness is the orientation with more power, and men generally have more power and are more dominant than women.

In relationships between heterosexuals, women accompany men.

They might also require protection and bearing from men. It might be acceptable for women to appear to be in charge in some settings, like the home.

However, practices that are inappropriate for women are not covered by this (Connell, 1987; 2000 Jackson; Bibbings, 2004).

It is essential to comprehend that this model of heteronormative career paths has both symbolic and practical effects.

Relationships between women and men are not always guaranteed to follow heterosexual norms, and certainly not everyone would view them as ideals, as women's activist heterosexuality pundits do (see Rich, 1980; Jackson, 1999). Notwithstanding, it is fundamental to look at the administrative force of ideal gentility developments while inspecting talks of conduct that conflicts with womanliness' limits.

The "muse" side of the extremity is in accordance with perceived hetero refinement here and there. Women take orders from men and become drawn in with murder due to their relationship with men. Even though this may implicate them in behavior that violates feminine norms, they are frequently perceived as having been duped, brainwashed, or coerced into participating (Morrissey, 2003).

Their actions thus fail to convey their true nature. Alternately, a comprehensible application of the female gender role is women's willingness to assist their male partners, particularly when those partners themselves do not actively engage in violence. In the part that preceded this one, we took a gander at how criminal science has checked female wrongdoing out. Naffine (1987) says that many crimes committed by women are considered feminine when they involve helping others or stealing goods. Comparisons can help shape women's support for rough behavior, even if it comes as a surprise.

As a result, the muse is a normal woman rather than a deviant.

The depiction, on the other hand, is more muddled than it first appears.

One subset of this category is referred to as the "muse" to convey the idea that women may appear to have inspired their male partners to commit violent acts. Women may be viewed as less important than the killing itself and as acting under a man's influence, but their sexual relationship can be made to be the primary cause of the crime. Right when murder is depicted to go probably as a portrayal of prominent manliness, it is the responsibility of ladies to help with conveying this power.

On the "plan" side of the spectrum, women are encouraged to be the driving force behind a group of female and male murderers. It is possible that the woman has manipulated the man or persuaded him to do what she wants because this portrayal portrays the woman as the scheming and plotting individual. It is acknowledged that the woman's longings energize the exercises, even though she is not exactly obligated to or even a part of the dangerous mercilessness. These cravings might be seen as sexual or material, as will be examined corresponding to explicit cases. is contrary to the customary female job for ladies to overshadow men, particularly in an unfeminine field like murder. According to Head servant (1999), the framework for normalizing heterosexuality is challenged by the notion that women rule and control men. It also undermines the acceptable structure of heterosexual relationships, Jackson (1999) claims, as well as the desire that is influenced by manly sexuality and activity.

The mastermind is, as a result, a perilous and unsettling figure. As Clytemnestra5, driving forces exhibit bizarre behavior that elevates them above natural womanliness and makes them appear almost magically malicious. This portrayal has the potential to become a significant representation of female risk due to Myra Hindley, who is examined below (Birch, 1993; Storrs, 2006). It's possible that mastermind discourse and the depiction of masculine women in the preceding chapter overlap. Also, it was contended that Rose West, who was portrayed as having a strange, "manly" sexuality, was liable for the killings of ladies and little kids in Gloucestershire.

The dream/engineer polarity as often as possible has different sides that are challenging to recognize. A similar lady is depicted in various ways, either as a helper or as a casualty of her male accomplice, or as the underhanded one who carried out the wrongdoing or violations and took advantage of her accomplice's sexual craving for her. The reason for this lack of separation is that the opposing sides of the polarity are inextricably linked to one another. The fantasy follows the virtuoso who plans masculine approach to acting. The women that are developed as a result of these discussions become liminal figures as a result of these two depictions sliding over one another. They are hazardous considering the way that it very well might be difficult to pick their genuine degree of association or impact at last.

In turn, this makes the muse/mastermind dichotomy more likely to emerge in particular historical instances that cause social anxiety. In Western social orders, the male-female sexual relationship is so crucial to orientation that when it fails completely, it is seen as a sign of a larger social breakdown.

Myra Hindley It is extremely uncommon for women to be involved in abduction, sexual abuse, or torture-related murders. Be that as it may, occurrences in which ladies participate in such lead with male accomplices ordinarily become irrefutably factual and notable. Even though women like Myra Hindley are unusual in real life, their stories are so important that it's important to look at how they are portrayed in orientation development. The majority of women convicted of manslaughter kill either their own child or a male accomplice, despite the fact that the phrase "ladies who kill" is likely to conjure up images of shocking homicides committed by women, such as those committed by Myra Hindley and Rose West.

Even after Myra Hindley passed away in 2002, her status in Britain remained nearly legendary. She has been portrayed in pop songs, television shows, and crafts, all in front of an audience. She received media attention from her 1966 conviction until her death (Schone, 2000; Grant, 2004). Myra Hindley was found guilty of murdering two children and harboring and reassuring her boyfriend, Ian Brady, who had also killed a third child. Brady had also killed a child. At the time, she was 23 years old. In 1986, she confessed to having been involved in the deaths of two additional youths and assisted the police in locating one of the victims' remains (Birch, 1993; After serving 36 years in prison, Myra passed away (Whitty and Murphy, 2006). The trial judge suggested that she serve 25 years in 1966. The Home Secretary lessened her sentence to "whole life" in 1990, 24 years after her basic conviction (Murphy and Whitty, 2006).

Myra Hindley and Ian Brady are insinuated as the Fields Executioners due to the way that they covered their setbacks on the fields near Manchester, England. Pauline Reade, then 16 years old, was their first victim in 1963. Myra's husband, David Smith, saw Ian smother 17-year-old Edward Evans and called the police on him and Myra in 1965 (Birch, 1993). According to Murphy and Whitty (2006), the police presented disturbing images and a sound recording of 10-year-old Lesley Ann Downey during their investigation. Birch (1993) says that the police also found Nazi memorabilia and pictures of Myra and Ian having sex. It was asserted in court that the killings were associated with whimsical and twisted sexual way of behaving.

Despite her involvement in their selection, blood removal, and execution, Myra's involvement in the homicides is unclear. Her depictions have fundamentally centered around her as a female lowlife who took part in kid murders as an unnatural "hostile to mother" (Birch, 1993; The Saints; Whitty and Murphy, 2004–2006) Myra Hindley's development, on the other hand, has been dualistic. The prosecution argued that Myra was a cover-up for Ian's murder. According to Whitty and Murphy, he had manipulated her and undermined her. She is portrayed as either Pygmalion, who adheres to the script and wishes, or Ian Brady's Woman Macbeth, who arranges the homicides and is "substantially more significantly insidious" than he was, according to Cameron and Frazer (1987). Myra Hindley, another victim in the original, is forced out of dread to support Ian Brady's manly vengeance. In the second, she undergoes transformation into a legendary beast that poses a threat to humanity and femininity.

Myra's direction character must be created with a restricted measure of meandering aimlessly assets past the fantasy/plan division. At the point when it recognizes a lady's complicity in the sexual murders of kids, from which she might have determined satisfaction, it is challenging to track down a language that doesn't fall into wretchedness. The dichotomous portrayal of her renders her distant, making it challenging to identify the "true" Myra Hindley. Birch (1993) suggests that Myra's appearance as a young woman contributes to this mystery, particularly in the well-known police photo taken after her arrest, in which she has peroxide-blonde hair and dark eyes. For a 23-year-old working-class woman in the 1960s, Myra's blonde hair and attention to her appearance were common. However, the styled haircut was interpreted as a disguise—an unsuccessful attempt by a sneaky, large woman to conceal her true essence—and as a twisted display of excessive gentility (Birch, 1993).

Karla Homolka and her male accomplice, Paul Bernardo, were linked to seizing, torture, and sexual abuse-related murders, just like Myra Hindley. Throughout their relationship, which began in 1987 when she was 17 and he was 23, she was mistreated and beaten. After getting married in 1991, Karla and Paul lived in a pink clapboard house in St. Catherines, Ontario, Canada. Karla owned up to the police her commitment in the killings of Leslie Mahaffy and Kristen French, two secondary school young women whose analyzed bodies had been encased in concrete and thrown into Lake Ontario, and she left Paul in January 1993 right after getting a particularly serious beating. She also told the police that her sister Tammy, who was 16 years old at the time of her death in 1990, had been seduced by the couple with opiates so they could attack her (Riehle, 1996; According to Kilty and Frigon (2007), in February 1993, Paul was taken into custody by the authorities in connection with a string of rapes that he had committed in the Scarborough area of Toronto.

Nonetheless, the state carried him to preliminary for the killings of three little kids by utilizing Karla's proof. In exchange for a plea bargain in which she admitted to two counts of manslaughter, Karla provided specific details regarding the murders. Leslie Mahaffy and Kristen French were arrested, and Karla was associated with Kristen's catch. Before Paul killed the young women, they were kept locked down for a couple of days and presented to sexual abuse. Karla was released from prison in 2005 after serving a 12-year sentence. Paul was found guilty in 1995 of adding the charge of murder against Leslie, Kristen, and Tammy Homolka in 1994. His sentence was life in prison. Videotapes showing the three girls being sexually assaulted and raped were discovered after Karla was found guilty of manslaughter. They demonstrated that she was participating in the abuse with all of her energy (Riehle, 1996; Morrissey, 2003; Karla Homolka's improvement as a Paul Bernardo loss and a hazardous, prey-pursuing partner delivers her obscure (Kilty and Frigon, 2007).

Morrissey (2003) expresses that in her own assertion, she said that she was a "battered mate" with little command over her life. She focused on that Paul controlled her and that she was an overcomer of his mercilessness and feared for her prosperity.

Karla answered that she realized Paul planned to kill Kristen and Leslie and dreaded he would kill her when she was inquired as to why she didn't assist Kristen and Kristen with getting away. Karla also maintained that in order to avoid being beaten by Paul, as she appeared to do on camera, she had to pretend that she did not enjoy the rape and sexual abuse of the victims. Clinical proof of her exploitation, as per Kilty and Frigon (2007), was introduced at her preliminary to help her case that she had little command over the killings. Karla's role as another of Paul's victims and any notion that she was physically pleased by her support of the assault and sexual abuse of the individuals in question vanished when she became one of Paul's casualties.

According to the fantasy, Paul, a charming young man who was trained as a clerk, married Karla, a charming young blonde woman from a common background. Morrissey (2003) claims that he was capable of dominating, controlling, and recruiting her to participate in his heinous crimes. Because of Karla and Paul's supposed standard appearance as an engaging hetero couple, the violations were surely alluded to as the "Barbie and Ken" murders (Riehle, 1996).

In addition to the obvious compatibility between Karla and Paul, this superficial attraction further emphasized her dichotomy as a risky, manipulative woman and a frail, defrauded one. Karla did not develop into the genius that led to the wrongdoings; Instead, she was made to be someone who could control the overall arrangement of rules, which was how she showed off her comedy skills. It was believed that her approval of the Battered Lady Issue (BWS) and the solicitation deal, which saved her from a murder conviction and a life sentence, demonstrated her ability to manipulate others. This side of the contention keeps up with that Karla was saved all out discipline for activities for which she was similarly capable (Kilty and Frigon, 2007).

According to Morrissey (2003), Paul had fulfilled some of the "normal" heterosexual man's fantasies, such as filming and having sex with two women simultaneously.

However, the fact that a woman would take part in the crimes was extremely unusual, and it was difficult to imagine Karla's involvement being anything other than horrifying.

Morrissey (2003) claims that there is no evidence Karla was a lesbian; Instead, it was accepted that controlling the younger girls and pleasing Paul was enjoyable for her.

According to Kilty and Frigon (2007), Karla's apparent prudent use of propriety was also interpreted as evidence of her controllable nature. Because her younger sister, Tammy, trusted her, she had the option of buying Tammy for Paul. Paul and Karla kidnapped Kristen French when they asked for directions. Paul's defense attorney referred to Karla as a "Venus fly trap" who conned the girls into their fate (Morrison, 2003, p. 146). It was possible to kidnap Kristen French because of her pretty appearance and demeanor. This thought suggests that Karla was a blonde sex offender who was both a sexual assailant and a target of sexual desire.

Despite Paul's ability to create extreme fantasies that were clearly masculine, Karla's participation rendered her dangerous and inaccessible. How much she was either a willing colleague or a compelled difficulty stay confounding.

Socially, ladies' contribution in kid and juvenile sexual killings is viewed as an indication of more profound social issues. Because they are the limit markers of public culture, women's unethical or irreverent behavior is especially upsetting. Right when Myra

Hindley and Ian Brady were seen as unforgivable in 1966, highlight essayists like Pamela Hansford Johnson (1967), who covered the introduction for the Standard Message, were worried that their awful ways of behaving showed what could end up peopling from the generally confused middle class when they were acquainted with contemplations that were annihilating. The couple's interest in Nazism and De Sade's "pornography" seemed to highlight the risks of introducing these ideas to unprepared minds. Due to the broad accessibility of erotic entertainment and ideas of sexual freedom, Johnson was especially worried about the chance of an expansion in the quantity of wrongdoings carried out against kids. In his 1968 novel The Sleep of Reason, Johnson's husband C. P. Snow loosely based a murder trial on the Moors Murders, despite the fact that both of the murderers were women. The homicide of a youthful individual fills in as an image for the obscured side of this new very much arranged request, drawing predominantly on class mobility, mass readiness, and sexual open door.

When evaluating this anxiety, the social setting at the time must be taken into consideration (Storrs, 2004; Borowitz, 2005). Shortly after the Second World War, advanced education, the development of additional qualifications offered by the government assistance state, new levels of opulence among working people, and widespread optional education had altered England's social scene. It is no longer reasonable to expect the typical person to "know their place." Class distinctions and sexual norms were also changing in the 1960s (Marwick, 1998). The Fields Murders were translated as an unquestionable admonishing of this change's expected results.

In the 1990s, Karla Homolka and Paul Bernardo developed their own distinct specters in Canada. Karla and her parents appeared to have been close, and both appeared to have been raised in nice, middle-class homes. According to Riehle (1996), they appeared to be a charming couple who lived in a small town on the shores of Lake Ontario and seemed happy and successful. By the 1990s, it was common knowledge that sexual fervor was linked to previous episodes of neglect and abuse. Criminal women were viewed as coming from unstable and undervalued backgrounds, according to Kilty and Frigon (2007). It appeared that Paul and Karla had quiet, typical childhoods. Karla's working-class, two-parent family background made these encounters seem mysterious, despite Paul's brutal treatment of her. Paul Bernardo and Karla Homolka raised the alarming possibility that "common" people might not be the same as "unpleasant, hazardous evildoers." Their deeds recommended that a serene town in Canada was home to an evil underground association.

This was socially troubling because Canadians frequently compared Canada to the more violent United States by highlighting its "cautious weapon regulations" and the "solidity and well-being" of its urban areas (Gilbert, 2006, p. 297). The cases of Paul Bernardo and Karla Homolka suggested that there was less security in the cultural divide between the two countries.

Despite the fact that sexuality is a significant component of the dream/engineer division because it depends on the possibility of a heterosexual connection between the lady and man who kill, sexuality has a rambling appearance that is not limited to sexual homicide. The relationship between the murderers is more significant than the manner of the crime. This trend also manifests itself in offenses committed without justification, retaliation, or financial gain. Karla Homolka and Myra Hindley debated the ultimate mystery surrounding women who are either constructed as victims, manipulative schemers, or con artists for their male partners. The primary purpose can break down the femme fatale's talk, which depicts the dangerous, mysterious woman in film noir (Doane, 1991).

The following section discusses the other notable instances in which genre-based narratives appeared.

Martha Beck, a 29-year-old woman, and Raymond Fernandez, a 34-year-old man, were blamed in 1949 for Janet Fay's death in Sovereigns, New York. Janet Fay was a 66-year-old widow to whom Raymond was locked up. Up until their execution in 1951, Martha and Raymond were held in Sing. (Knox, 1998), their case caused controversy. Raymond met ladies through individual paper commercials known as "Forsaken Hearts" clubs. He either persuaded them to wed him or procured their trust so they would give him money or assets. While traveling the world, he and Martha, his girlfriend, posed as siblings. Due to the possibility of killing a woman named Delphine Cutting and her 2-year-old daughter Rainelle, the couple was stranded in Michigan. They made confessions, with Martha admitting that she drowned Rainelle in the bathtub, according to reports. However, after they admitted to the murder of Nassau County resident Janet Fay, Martha and Raymond were extradited to New York. The case against the death penalty was eventually dropped in Michigan, which did not have it (Knox, 1998; 2002, Shipman) Despite media speculation that Martha and Raymond might be responsible for a variety of homicides, only the death of Janet Fay was viewed as Martha and Raymond's fault.

Martha was depicted as the essential culprit of the wrongdoing in both the underlying examination and ensuing veritable bad behavior and imaginative renderings of the case (Knox, 1998). Raymond changed his security from ferocity part of the way through the start and really attempted to bring down the expense of his circumstance to progress in a brief time, investing him in subordinate effort in the killing. News reports referred to Martha as "Fat Martha" (Knox, 1998, p. 87) and a "200 pound divorced person" (Shipman, 2002, p. 72) due to her weight. The discussion she had about her weight underscored both her accepted strength and anomaly as well as her control over Raymond.

They used Martha's anomaly as a definition of craziness in an effort to combat it. It was contended that her overweight foundation assumed a part in her lopsided mental state. Additionally, Martha's unusual sexual behavior was confirmed by the safeguard. When she was young, her sibling attacked her, and it was thought that her irregularity had caused her to have sexual problems. On the advice of a doctor, Martha and Raymond engaged in oral sex, which was portrayed as degenerate in court, in order for Martha to achieve orgasm. As per Knox (1998), the arraignment excused that Martha's eccentricities were proof of franticness right now rather of her terrible individual and profanity.

The romance genre was aware of Martha's actions, even though it was believed that Martha was superior to Raymond (Knox, 1998). Despite the fact that she was a large, mentally ill woman with bombed connections in her past, Raymond treated her better than she had in the past. As a result, her love for him became more apparent. This point of view demonstrates that

Martha assigned various women because she was lusting after them and anticipated that Raymond would no longer require her. The romance story continued while the "Lonely Hearts Killers" were awaiting execution in Sing Sing after letters between them were leaked to the media. Raymond was depicted as a reluctant and feeble legend, and Martha, an unusual and ugly lady, was utilized as a satire heartfelt champion. The case could also be made up using a film noir classification from a different time. Knox (1998) claims that this form of the story depicts Martha as a dangerous femme fatale who goes after her darling. Nevertheless, she wasn't a pretty blonde; rather, she was a bloated, frumpy divorcee.

Through popular genres of the time, the sensational case of the "Lonely Hearts Killers" could be told. Contrary to Karla Homolka and Myra Hindley, Martha Beck was depicted as a comedic character who, due to her physical appearance and background, made for a charming romantic heroine or femme fatale. However, readers of the paper were intrigued by the case because it addressed a number of contemporary issues. In the middle of the 20th century, it was common practice in the United States to say that people had been freed from the confines of an immaterial metropolitan scene and from the distant, predictable nature of modern life. This condition was attempted to be explained using sociological concepts like anomie (Merton, 1946, 1949). Martha Beck and Raymond Fernandez appeared to have capitalized on the alienating concept of contemporary life by focusing on lonely women with individual promotions. Foertsch (2008) claims that the "Lonely Hearts" murders took place in a nation that, following the Second World War, had become more powerful but also more culturally conservative and apprehensive, living with the atomic age's constant threat.

Bonnie Parker and Clyde Barrow may be the most well-known heterosexual couple murder cases in the United States due to Arthur Penn's 1967 film Bonnie and Clyde. They were members of a gang led by Clyde that killed approximately 12 people in the Midwest and south of the United States between 1932 and 1934. The majority of their victims were police officers, and they frequently ransacked supermarkets and service stations in small towns in search of generally insignificant sums of cash. Their most profitable theft netted less than $10,000 in profits. In 1934, they were snatched by police and killed (Potter, 1998; 2007 Hendley).

Bonnie and Clyde, notable thieves, were keenly conscious about their public picture. Bonnie took pictures of them presenting with weapons and composed works about their endeavors. Clyde's group was remarkable because of Bonnie's presence. They were a small group of con artists who were not very successful without her; However, her presence infused the group's narrative with romance (Hendley, 2007).

Bonnie needed level and was in her mid 20s. In contrast to Martha Beck, her appearance was viewed as engaging and female.

As per her mom, who composed a biography about Bonnie, she turned into a criminal because of her affection for Clyde (Potter, 1998). The primary foundation of their mythology is their relationship.

Bonnie is consistently portrayed as the fantasy side of the fantasy/plan extremity rather than as Clyde's setback by virtue of her little level and clear devotion to Clyde. Be that as it may, different understandings of the story have been offered, and the exact idea of Bonnie's contribution in the wrongdoings has been questioned. Some stories say that she told Clyde where to go and laughed as she killed two injured police officers (Hendley, 2007), while others say she never fired a shot. It is essential to comprehend the appeal of Bonnie and Clyde in 1930s America during the economic downturn. As a result of the Great Depression and the Wall Street Crash, Americans with lower socioeconomic status and a slightly middle class saw their lives become increasingly precarious. During a practically identical timeframe, zeroing in on news on radio and news reels had changed into a typical side interest for ordinary occupants. According to Potter (1998), stories about current criminals who oppose the state followed financially troubled metropolitan and rural Americans. In spite of their banditry on the pristine interstate roadways, which showed their resistance to power, Bonnie and Clyde missing the mark on political inspiration or coordinated resistance to state authority. People who encountered the police through forced evictions and arrests for unemployment and homelessness may have found the murder of police officers less objectionable (Potter, 1998), which is especially true for the Bonnie and Clyde story from the 1960s, which was portrayed in films as a heartfelt criminal team battling the state. The case was constructed using the American "road" genre, in which the protagonists embark on a quest, self-discovery, or escape (Primeau, 1996), The social pressures, such as Bonnie Parker's turn of events and the kind of killing she was associated with, contributed to an ideal portrayal. Bonnie made the adventures of the group led by Clyde Barrow more romantic by adding glitz and novelty. She was not portrayed as an unnatural woman, in contrast to Martha Beck, in spite of the way that her contribution in awful violations could challenge direction norms. Faye Dunaway made Bonnie Parker into a fashionable counterculture icon more than 30 years later when she played her in the movie Bonnie and Clyde (Hendin, 2004; Melossi) in 2008

Nervousness in regards to the violence of female connections is addressed by the fantasy's cerebrum extremity. If they are not piece players in serious

savage infringement, for instance, murder, then, at that point, they should the assault drive

force. This is in line with long-standing concerns regarding the feminine's potential for evil and indecipherability. Because of the impact that the male/female hetero organization has on regularizing orientation relations, connections that have inflicted damage or obliteration can act as an image for current tensions and disappointments. As the case of Bonnie Parker demonstrates, romanticized depictions can also be moved by serving as an illustration of current disappointment. This sometimes includes negative depictions of women and men participating in unusual homicides.

The hurt person Women's dissident experts have looked at guarantees and explanations for why women kill, taking into account female pathology, especially flawed science. For instance, women who killed their children younger than one year old when the mother was experiencing the effects of labor or lactation at the time were charged with a lesser crime than murder in the Child murder Demonstration of 1938 in Britain and Ribs (Kramar and Watson, 2006; Rapaport, 2006). Pre-Ladylike Confusion was effectively used to help a decreased responsibility monitor in specific ladies' crime starter assessments during the 1980s in Canada, the Unified Realm, and the Bahamas (Kendall, 1991; Rose, 2000). In North America, Australia, and New Zealand, expert evidence of BWS, a condition thought to be caused by domestic abuse, can be presented to support defenses of women who kill abusive partners (Schuller et al.,

2004; 2006, Melillo and Russell; Sutherland, 2006). BWS is a condition that mostly affects women and does not originate in the female body, unlike the monthly cycle or labor. These psychological explanations for women's homicide have focused women's extreme reactions on their tendency to deny women's connection and to pathologize socially lived experiences of abuse and child care.

There is no specific discussion of female embodied pathologies or madness constructions in this chapter. All things being equal, it checks out at the casualty's considerations, as odd instances of dangerous ladies. This is accomplished by focusing on women with personality disorders, particularly "psychopathic" ones, as well as related concepts of "dangerousness." Because they are mental disorders rather than illnesses, it is unclear whether personality disorders can be treated. Psychopathy is closely associated with hostility, a lack of trustworthiness, and a failure to recognize the full range of serious behavioral conditions. It is thought that people with these traits and little understanding of their condition are more likely to be risky or dangerous to others. According to Kozol et al., the psychopath or damaged personality fluctuates between mental health and illness. 1972). This liminality has the capacity to upset itself in light of the discussion of the causes of psychopathy and behavioral conditions (Moran, 1999;

2007) Royal College of Psychiatrists In the women's activist criminological grant on fierce women, which typically looks at the development of mental illness that is only experienced by women, the harmed person is a neglected area.

Men are bound to have psychopathy, serious behavioral conditions, and thoughts of the "risky wrongdoer," as per Kendall (2005). A damaged personality is not more common in females than in males. Notwithstanding, the gendered impacts of this talk are analyzed in this part according to surprising instances of female homicide. The concept of psychopathy, personality disorders associated with it, and shifting perceptions of danger will all be the subject of research. According to Halttunen (1998), the concept of the damaged personality and its connection to danger can be traced back to the nineteenth century, when secular rather than religious explanations were offered for human behavior that would have been considered "evil" in the past.

The development of the mental case Mental composition in the latter part of the 1800s and the beginning of the 1900s gives rise to the possibility of psychopathy. According to Pinel (1806), people acted "madness-like" or "morally off the wall" in a hasty, socially unacceptable manner for which they bore no responsibility. Moral franticness, as per Pritchard (1835), is a state of mind that is described by jumbled impact in individuals who have typical scholarly advancement. These individuals were presumably going to have criminal propensities that didn't change due to the gamble of discipline or their involvement in it. The concept of moral insanity was characterized by two characteristics that were later discovered to be flaws in conceptualizations of psychopathy and severe personality disorders. The first was the need to make a good decision when an unfortunate behavior was discovered.

According to Herve (2007), the next issue was a lack of definitional clarity, which meant that "ethical craziness" could refer to numerous socially unacceptable behaviors and characteristics.

The expressions "psychopathic person" and "psychopathic second rate" arose because of the discussion encompassing Pritchard's idea of moral madness (Craftsman, 2005). The psychopathy speculation emerged in American criminological writing during the 20th 100 years due to the treatment approach that governed penology in the US and Exceptional Britain up until the 1970s (Crossbeam, 1997).

Theories of psychopathy gained popularity, particularly in the middle of the twentieth century. In the 1950s, the term "maniac" became more common in psychological health and lay speech (Arrigo and Shipley, 2001), and the idea was certainly more apparent in psychiatric literature than it had ever been before (Raman, 1986).

In the twentieth century, a few filmmakers addressed the significance of psychopathy. The Veil of Mental soundness (1941), perhaps of Cleckley's most huge work, keeps on molding our impression of insane people. Cleckley argued that mental cases may appear to be appealing and keen from all perspectives. However, they fell short of expectations in terms of significant emotional responses and inclination or sympathy. He struggled that psychopathy could be made due. Regarding the mental case's capacity for change, Karpman (1941, 1946, and 1948) communicated a relative negativity. He proposed that maniacs' personal encounters were innocent because of their significant profound youthfulness.

They should not be seen as empty; rather, they should be seen as incapable of experiencing complex emotions like compassion, obligation, and sorrow. Because they were so young, it seemed like people with mental illnesses had poor judgment when it came to their strong and difficult reasons. The maniac only experiences "shortcircuited" emotions like dissatisfaction, delight, or displeasure, according to Arieti (1963, 1967).

Around the middle of the 20th century, it was thought that psychopathy, a behavioral condition distinguished by solitary tendencies, was strongly linked to wrongdoing. As per Johnstone (1996), sociopaths were the people who had confidence in the potential for change through treatment when they were past reclamation because of their imperfect person. As a result, psychopathy assisted in elucidating the most difficult aspects of treatment. Henderson's (1939) classification of psychopathic characters into three categories had an impact on the English perspective. The types lacked originality, aggression, and social skills. The socially awkward and psychopathic character had withdrawing tendencies and failed to marry and work normally without government assistance. "Feeble-mindedness," which was thought to indicate low social functioning, was thought to be associated with this label. According to Woodton (1959), the concept of lack was linked to a previous perspective on inherent deficiency that was enhanced by particular reproduction.

McCord and McCord (1964) emphasized the psychopath's socially inept personality and lack of emotion on the basis of previous research.

In addition, they emphasized that young, innocent people who want immediate gratification are maniacs. The McCords demonstrated that some individuals may have an innate tendency toward psychopathy, which may be initiated by parental exclusion. If children did not have the chance to bond with their parents, they would not be able to do so effectively.

Under the Psychological Need Exhibition of 1927, which replaced the 1913 task of "moral simpleton," moral defect was a characterization of mental flaws in Britain and Edges. "Psychopathic character" became a legitimate class under the Emotional well-being Demonstration of 1959, which altered mental health regulations. It was anything but a dysfunctional behavior, notwithstanding being named such (Williams et al., 1960).

Insane person can be disconnected into two classes: (According to Johnstone (1996), the Psychological Wellness Demonstration of 1983 maintains that psychopathic conditions are conditions for which patients may be expected to be admitted to a clinic assuming that clinical treatment can alleviate their condition. Walker and McCabe, 1973) the extremely careless and forceful

Analysis of the terms "sociopath" and "psychopathic character" in the twentieth century revealed that these were "wastebasket" terms for troublesome, simply bad people. Due to their lack of clinical specificity, they were unable to avoid becoming catch-alls for many socially inappropriate behaviors. It cast doubt on the legitimacy of the term psychopathic character if it could be so flexible (Biggs, 1955; 1959 Wallinga;

(1959, Wootton) Various terms began to offset psychopathy during the 1950s and 1960s. In 1952, the American Mental Connection consolidated a significance of sociopathy rather than psychopathy in the Suggestive and Verifiable Manual I.

Sociopaths are "tirelessly against social individuals" who are "consistently hard and greedy, showing stepped near and dear energy, with nonappearance of commitment," as communicated on page 46 of Herve (2007). " extreme behavioral condition showing a penchant toward crime" was referenced in the American Model Condemning Demonstration of 1963 (cited in Guttmacher, 1963, p. 381).

During the last 50% of the 20th hundred years, conversations of "psychopathic individual" were much of the time supplanted as a primary concern science and psychiatry by contemplations of serious lead issues. In the DSM III, these were categorized as constant circumstances in light of conduct characteristics rather than clinical disorders (1980). Anti-Social Personality Disorder (ASPD) replaced and expanded on the definitions of sociopathy in the DSM I. Psychopathy and ASPD share characteristics like impulsivity, aggression, and disordered affect. In spite of conflict in regards to whether the terms would be able or ought to be utilized reciprocally, it is every now and again recommended that most of maniacs can likewise be determined to have ASPD (Bunny, 1993;

Herve, 2007). Ten behavioral conditions are categorized into three groups in DSM IV (1994): erratic, irrational, and whimsical, and resistant to pressure. According to Lenzenweger and Clarkin (2004), ASPD is a personality disorder that is "impulsive-erratic." It is the one most frequently associated with danger and violent or criminal behavior.

Personality disorders are currently diagnosed with behavioral criterion-based psychological testing instruments. Lenzenweger and Clarkin (2004) say that this made these situations more specific and made them more legitimate. In any case, the value of behavioral condition diagnosis and whether these findings reveal a significant jumble rather than a socially unsatisfactory behavior is still up for debate (Moran, 1999). The term ASPD is as of now comprehensively more dedicated to

be used than psychopathy. In 1993, Hare's Psychopathy Checklist (PCL) and its revised version (PCL-R) rekindled scientific interest in psychopathy as a condition. Based on Cleckley's (1941) research into psychopaths, the PCL-R is a 20-characteristic clinical rating scale. Assumption, nonattendance of sympathy, impulsivity, and shallow sentiments are occasions of these. The checklist can be used by psychologists to diagnose psychopathy.

Therapeutically and lawfully, harmed characters are developed. It is possible to use different clinical terms in reverse in legitimate and well-known representations. As a result, when presented in court, a defense based on psychopathy or ASPD may not strictly adhere to psychological or psychiatric definitions. In literature, films, and television shows, the sociopath is frequently portrayed as a dangerous and dishonest figure. The social comprehension of psychopathy and serious conduct problems is upgraded by these portrayals.

Psychopathy, insidiousness, and danger Conditions like psychopathy and ASPD make people feel powerless to change the situation. Because it is believed that they lack a rational or explicable motivation, it can be challenging to predict their violent behavior. Despite the fact that they appear to have a problem, these people frequently come across as difficult to treat or change. Bricklayer et al. state that, These credits are very similar to notions of deception, which are typically interpreted as portraying or expressing non-human actions

(Bricklayer et al., 2002).

Psychopathy and senseless lead conditions can fill in as comparable words for devilish in quantifiable and authentic settings. According to Mason and colleagues (2002), mental health professionals at a high-security psychiatric hospital in England considered some mentally ill violent offenders to be evil. Unsettles' (2004) investigation focuses on the connection that exists between psychopathy, ASPD, and evil in Australian courts. She asserts that by analyzing conditions that share the characteristics of evil, the courts are able to make moral decisions regarding vicious wrongdoers under the guise of judicious and logical language. Since they are viewed as being especially dangerous, these crooks get crueler sentences.

Kozol and co. state that psychopathy and ASPD risk have significant strengths. 1972). Control measures have been around for quite a while. Prins (2002) claims that English law increased the riskiness of the poor and wanderers from the Elizabethan period onward. A sense of danger was created when the criminally disadvantaged were shown to be close to danger. This was applied to individuals who seemed, by all accounts, to be common yet were obviously inspired to carry out awful killings. Experts utilized the ideas of moral frenzy examined in the principal area to make sense of such infringement (Foucault, 1978). As a result, it became obvious that madness could pursue feelings while remaining conscious of thought and mindfulness.

Criminal anthropologists argued, in the latter part of the nineteenth century, that a person's level of danger to society was more important than their legal responsibility. It was important to recognize people whose chance could be diminished through treatment and the individuals who were impervious to intercession (for whom they suggested passing or long haul detainment). In the latter part of the nineteenth century, there was a possibility that the state should be responsible for reducing and controlling risks to everyone (Foucault, 1978; Pratt, 2000). This included threats from particular individuals. The term "perilous being" was coined by the Global Association of Punitive Regulation in 1905, around the same time that there was less resistance to mental and humanistic approaches to dealing with criminal behavior (Van Hamel, 1911; Foucault, 1978). Even though not all of them would be considered "dangerous," the English and Welsh Prevention of Crime Act of 1908 established preventive detention for repeat offenders. This arranged the meaning of public security.

By the middle of the 20th century, psychopaths and people with personality disorders were at the center of concerns regarding the necessity of using indefinite detention to safeguard the public from dangerous criminals. By the 1950s, sexual sociopath regulations had been sanctioned in certain US purviews. The meaning of confinement for treatment was every now and again talked about in North American and European regulation. Guttmacher (1963) claims that Danish courts could suggest "psychopathic detainment" for an endless timeframe in offices staffed by exceptionally prepared faculty. In England and Wales, the Mental Health Act of 1959 made it possible to define "psychopathic personality disorder" and mandate hospitalization. The Drawn Out Sentence was established in 1961 by the Law Enforcement Act for individuals who were thought to pose a threat to society (Prins, 2002).

Attempts to control people with personality disorders or

psychopathy in the middle of the 20th century tended to believe that education and treatment could aid in recovery. The US Model Denouncing Demonstration of 1963 described dangerous wrongdoers as "encountering a super social condition showing a propensity for wrongdoing" (referenced in Guttmacher, 1963, p. 381). The Act stipulated that dangerous offenders would be given sentences that were sufficient for rehabilitation but could be increased to 30 years if they did not complete their rehabilitation. According to Flood (1963), the concept of the offender and the potential threat to the general public were more significant than the actual wrongdoing.

The corrective welfarism of the time, which recognized that the majority of criminals could benefit from treatment and education, was reflected in the Model Condemning Demonstration's approach (Laurel, 2001).

In the United States, Great Britain, Australia, and New Zealand, attitudes toward dangerous criminals increased and laws became more stringent in the latter half of the 20th century. Increasing numbers of criminals were receiving significantly longer sentences. Pratt (2000) claims that, for instance, California's "three strikes" laws led to life sentences for individuals who were not necessarily thought to be mentally dangerous. "The organization of risk started to accept a certainly undeniable part in the action of the policing, and public protection became significantly positively a need," writes Kemshall (2004). Mullen (1999) says that controversial proposals for indefinite detention in England and Wales focused on "dangerous severely personality disordered" individuals. This type of detention could be approved solely based on the results of an expert evaluation, even if the individual has not committed a crime. In the latter part of the 1990s and the middle of the 21st century, the use of uncertain sentences for sexual and violent offenders increased in England and elsewhere (Kemshall and Maguire, 2001; Tracker, 2005) When studying hurt character talk about women who kill, it is essential to keep in mind threats. Since both homicide and murder can bring about extensive times of detainment without unique measures, the issues relating to the utilization of uncertain sentences are fairly particular from those relating to manslaughter. Obviously, the use of jail for of public security shows the improvement of the unsafe reprehensible party as a dangerous picture.

It is difficult to compare the sentences that various ladies received due to differences in rehearsal times and locations. It is additionally hard to clearly dissect choices because of the variety of criminal regulations.

However, in order to ascertain whether a condition like psychopathy or severe personality disorder is connected to public safety, the discursive construction of various cases can be examined.

This section focuses on three notable young women and women who were found to have mental or serious behavioral issues. It looks at their liminal status as "neither sane nor insane" and the clear ludicrous anxiety they caused through their bad behaviors. According to Halttunen (1998), in order to comprehend "evil," discussions of social failure always turn to the damaged personality. These may focus on the conditions that prompted a risky or harmed individual or on the absence of casualty insurance that permitted the damage to occur.

In 1968, Mary Ringer was seen as to blame for the killings of 4-year-old Martin Brown and 3-year-old Brian Howe, both of whom lived in her space, in Newcastle, north-east England. Martin's case is one of the most well-known examples of a child under the age of 14 being held responsible for the deaths of other children.6 In May 1968, her body was found in a neglected house. Brian's body was discovered on some waste ground after two months, raising suspicions that he had passed on unintentionally. On December 6, 1968, he had been fatally cut with scissors and a razor, according to The Times.

The pathologist gathered that Brian had likely been stifled by a youngster in view of the impacts on his neck, which recommended less power than an adult would utilize (Sereny, 1995). The police were able to make a connection between Martin's and Brian's deaths due to the absence of traces on Brian's neck. Around 1200 youngsters' explanations were gathered in Scotswood, the Newcastle neighborhood where the passings had happened.

Mary Chime, who was 11 years of age, and Norma Ringer, who was 13 years of age, offered problematic expressions. Despite the fact that they shared a last name and lived close to one another, they were not related. Mary reported to the professionals that she had witnessed an 8-year-old boy playing with scissors and slicing Brian Howe. It was not clarified the way that the scissors had harmed Brian. The police checked out the child Mary mentioned, but they refused to let him in. The two young women laid the blame for Brian's choke on one another after Mary and Norma made additional declarations.

They were also faulted for killing Martin Brown and killing him as well (Sereny, 1995).

To ensure that Mary was psychopathic during the preliminary, the guard called two experts to verify their credentials.

According to the essential specialist, this was portrayed as hostility, lack of shame or sorrow, and lack of compassion for others. He looked over Mary's basically dull discussion of the young men's ends, which suggested this condition. According to Sereny (1995, p. 164), the subsequent specialist stated that Mary was "extremely dangerous" and had a serious character confusion. Mary had an impact on Norma when she was younger, the defense argued. What's more, they alluded to Mary as "insidious" and "evil" and accentuated her knowledge and control abilities. Mary was compared to a "Svengali" by the prosecution, who said she was "strong, shocking, fierce, unequipped for lament" and "a young woman, furthermore, had of a decision character, with a truly astounding information and a degree of guilefulness that is basically terrifying."

Norma was released from both murders, and Mary was held accountable for the homicide because her liability was reduced. The selected power said in his sentence that Mary was "risky" and addressed a "extraordinarily grave bet to various children" (Sereny, 1995, p. 187) (The Times, December 18, 1968). They were eligible for a hospital bed due to their psychopathic disorder diagnosis; Nevertheless, none of the facilities met their requirements. The adjudicator gave Mary a life sentence, which was fair considering that she would only be released when it was safe to do so. According to Sereny (1995), she was transferred to the Special Unit of the Red Bank Approved School in Lancashire, which had previously been restricted to boys only.

She was likewise a youngster who had killed different kids, and her belled direction affected how she was depicted in talk. At this, there were feelings of repulsiveness. Mary was also regarded as a crushed child, despite having a psychopathic social condition that put her in a few spots of mental sufficiency and frenzy. She used words that are synonyms for "sly" during her preliminary, such as "psychopathic," "perilous," and "mischievous." Mary was depicted for the situation inclusion as an "deceptive birth" and a "horrendous seed" in view of imaginary harrowing tales of risky youngsters (Sereny, 1995, p. 167). Mary's wrongdoings appeared to be significant at the time. She was a psychopath, and experts didn't know much about her past at this point (Sereny, 1998). They did know that her mother had sabotaged her as a child and used her badly (Sereny, 1998).

The event, like Mary Ring, seemed to address the moral decay of England in the late 1960s from a moderate perspective, which made it disturbing. Relating to Myra Hindley, it was referred to that the changing social scene of the time conveyed with it the dread that society would collapse if "ordinary" standards of goodness and commitment were broken. Society was worried about this.

Mary, according to Jackson and Scott (1999), was a child's representation of what might be coming, and Britain's "tolerant" society appeared to have few opportunities. The "stunning story" of the case was seen from the finish of the 1960s close by famous occasions like the Altamont Festivity and the Manson Family murders, which happened in the US in 19698 and addressed the "outcome" of the 1960s (Pursue, 2002, p. 95). As per Beck (1992), the ladies in the accompanying two cases decided to be orderlies and exemplified the bet loath attitudes of the late twentieth hundred years.

Genene Jones In Texas, Genene Jones started working as a substitute clinical regulator in the 1970s. She worked at the

Pediatric Emergency Unit at the Bexar Area Clinical Center from 1978 to 1982. During that time, it became clear that while she was there, a disproportionately high number of the babies she took care of went through multiple cardiac or respiratory arrests. Additionally, an unusually high number of fatalities were observed by the Unit. After Genene's coworkers noticed the unusual patterns of arrests and deaths associated with her shifts, the hospital gathered a group of outside medical professionals to examine her records. Genene should not have been reported to the police because the panel found insufficient evidence of homicide. According to Furbee (2006), the hospital only allowed registered nurses to work in the Unit. She was therefore denied employment.

In September 1982, Genene got a new job at a pediatric office that was 60 miles from the Bexar Territory Clinical Center. Her patients went into a prolonged respiratory arrest once more. A 15-month-old young woman kicked the pail directly following getting a mixture from Genene ensuing to working for a really long time at the new concentration. Concerns were communicated with respect to the respiratory catches of her patients because of the absence of a vial of the muscle relaxant succinylcholine chloride. In 1984, she was blamed for the death of a 15-month-old young woman, and the following year, she was blamed for harming another youngster by giving them muscle relaxants (Thunder, 2002; Furbee, 2006). According to Lucy and Aitken (2002), the court admitted evidence from previous suspicious incidents during Genene's murder trial, which resulted in her 99-year prison sentence.

Bunny (1993) uses Genene's case to frame a piece of

psychopathy; ability to trick and manipulate others. Rabbit argues that Genene was a well-prepared liar who was completely prepared to alter details about her past while describing her life in light of the essayist Elkind's 1990 work The Passing Development. According to Elkind (1990), Genene is frequently depicted as having harmed and killed young people in her effort to establish herself as the hero of the situation and due to the manner in which she selected a melancholy comedy from the most well-known strategy for attempting to reestablish them. Both of these factors contribute to the perception that Genene committed these acts. Elkind says that Genene did this with an end goal to set up a good foundation for herself as the legend of the circumstance. Kocsis and Irwin, 1998) She argued that the preliminary had no immediate evidence against her and that she had not administered lethal doses of succinylcholine to the children. Mental clarifications regarding the appropriate setting for the situation were therefore not discussed. In any case, genuine criminal and academic writing frequently depict Genene as psychopathic or suffering from severe behavioral issues. Moreover, Elkind (1990) recommends Munchausen's Condition As a substitute (MSbP) as a potential clarification for her hurting small kids, which will be examined more meticulously underneath.

In February 1991, Beverley Allitt started working as a short-term enrolled paediatric nurse at Grantham and Kesteven General Hospital in Lincolnshire, England. On her ward, there was a suspicious rise in the number of child deaths and cardiac and pulmonary arrests in the few months following her employment. Before their aspiratory capture, one youngster's after death assessment uncovered that they had gotten various insulin infusions. None exists.

Individuals you, me, we all are basically friendly creatures. Let potentially run wild, we will generally look for each other's organization — intellectually, genuinely, profoundly. You can place few individuals in an enormous space, and in a brief time frame they will bunch, looking to see, hear and contact each other.

It does not appear that being around other people is sufficient. On the everyday level, we, as people, will generally coordinate off looking for more than to simply "hang out" with arbitrary bipeds. We appear to have to experience passionate feelings for, be infatuated and share love. Since we as a whole appear to sort of need exactly the same things, you would figure bringing together and meet each other's common needs would be somewhat simple. But have you ever noticed that the more intelligent and sophisticated we get, the more difficult it seems to be to do the things in our lives that should be easy? I hear from people all the time that, for some reason, they just can't seem to find another person who is willing to share the words "we" and "us," much less put their boots under their beds and start filing joint tax returns. They let me know that they can't get a date and assuming that they do, it's either with some mouth-breather they genuinely want to believe that they at no point ever find in the future or a respectable person who won't get back to, either in light of the fact that he would rather not or is apprehensive his significant other could figure it out. Subsequently, they simply lounge around watching the window hangings blur.

As a couple of portions from your messages and letters show, the majority of you are keeping a comical inclination:
You may be in a better or worse situation than some of those women, but it's time to change things up and get what you really want.
We are about to significantly alter that if you are unable to fix the guy you got or find the man you want. Assuming that you're up around evening time asking why everyone around you, with the exception of you, is in extraordinary connections, getting ready for marriage, getting hitched, having children and zooming right along throughout everyday life, then, at that point, you and I are going to change that in a significant manner. In the event that you're not finding that unique individual who can illuminate you from the back to front, you are getting bamboozled, and we're certainly going to fix that. There's something off about something. Something is messed up. What aggravates it is that I accept with extraordinary assurance that this unique somebody exists. He is out there. You might have previously met him. You might even be in a relationship with him but are unable to take it to the next level, or you might be married to him but the spark has begun to fade.

To get the relationship you need, you must take a fair, even ruthless, see what's happening and what's turning out badly. You must be willing to alter your activities.

Simply a note to be certain that I'm extremely clear on a certain something: I'm going to let you in on certain mysteries and methodologies, expecting that you have concluded that you need to track down the ideal person for you. I don't currently accept, nor have I at any point accepted, that any lady must be hitched or have a man in her life to be entire, finished or crucially alive. If you find the right man, having a man in your life can be beneficial. It's beneficial to need and have a sweetheart or spouse (not simultaneously, obviously). However, this is not a requirement for you. Getting hitched isn't something you should do.

In this fast-paced day and age in our highly transient society, with its high divorce rate, the task of creating a strong and rewarding relationship may sound intimidating or even overwhelming, assuming that finding the right man is what you want. Allow me to guarantee you, it doesn't need to be. In point of fact, what we are about to do will be more entertaining than the law should permit. Knowing that every day could be the day you meet the person of your dreams, the person with whom you will spend the rest of your life, is so exciting and fun. No one can say with any certainty assuming the following conference you have, the following client you serve or the following corner you turn will place you before that very individual! Because of this, life is thrilling; It doesn't really matter to me what your identity is! Particularly in the event that out of nowhere you are done staggering along carelessly, yet rather have the right stuff, capacities, plans and techniques to get it going! You are going to become amazing at relating. You are about to attain your "black belt" in the relationship. Then you will glance back at what you used to do and simply shake your head.

Allow me to get us going by letting you know two things that I know for outright, drop-absolutely sure. First: on the off chance that you don't have what you really need in a relationship, then you are correct, something is truly off-base. But the crucial part is as follows: The problem is not you. I rehash, the issue isn't you. You are not a terrible individual. You are not neglecting to get a magnificently compensating relationship since you are not deserving of it. As a matter of fact, I accept, to the outright center of my spirit, that you are going to find a colossal mystery, as a matter of fact, I accept it is the trick of the trade in your life: YOU. This mystery isn't just being stowed away from individuals you see consistently, bond with or fantasy about wedding, it is being kept from you.

The second fact that I am absolutely certain of is that you are not thinking clearly or playing the game effectively; if not you would have what you need. We'll manage that in Section 4, "Single — There Are No Mishaps," since you are a meriting and quality potential relationship accomplice, yet you clearly don't have the foggiest idea how to get in the game or play the game once you do.

It is, indeed, a game. Some way or another or another, individuals have concluded that searching for adoration is some massively serious interaction that should be drawn closer with worship and etiquette. I surmise I ought not be so shocked since reality is normally connected with frantic circumstances and "urgency" is a word I frequently hear from all kinds of people in regards to their affection lives. I concur that choosing a soul mate and going with the choice to walk the passageway is a choice of gravity and merits the greatest possible level of in thought, supplication and thought. But getting there is a game, and if you want to win, you have to play it loosely and have fun. You must play the game without sweat-soaked palms or you won't ever get what you are searching for.

Saying that dating and relating is, to some degree to start with, a game doesn't imply that it is unimportant or pointless. Depend on it; I'm looking at rolling out a significant improvement in your life, explicitly your adoration life. Now is the right time to be a champ. Now is the ideal time to begin being a lady rather than a bridesmaid.

Consider it, the issue must be something other than you. Don't you know ladies who are, as you would see it, not quite as intriguing as you, not generally so savvy as you, not as cherishing and mindful and giving as you, not so charming or alluring as you, however yet they have an incredible relationship accomplice while you sit at home conversing with your houseplants? Why? Perhaps they just got visually impaired fortunate, yet I'm wagering they have what they need and what you wish you had on the grounds that they know how to play the game better compared to you do.

I realize that there are additionally ladies out there that you simply love to detest, in light of the fact that they appear to have everything going on. They're youthful, fit, stick-flimsy, lively and charming. You're thinking, "How would I rival that?" You stand in front of the mirror in your bathroom and say, "Look at my hair! Observe my hips! I have legs like stumps! My eyes are excessively far separated! This is the hereditary treachery that is my heritage! I'm bound to kick the bucket alone!" Indeed, wake up! I can guarantee you that you don't need or should be some glamorous lady model that spends her days on the runway. She might be starving at home or throwing up the dinner she just ate, looking in the mirror, and saying the same or worse things as you do. Also, I can't perceive you the number of men that I've heard check out at those ladies and say "For mercy's sake! I've seen more meat on tusks! She requires additional time at the buffet.

Assuming you're sitting at home hounding on yourself with an unending rundown of self-basic put-downs, then, at that point, I ensure that others, including men, will find it undeniably challenging to see esteem in you since you are concealing it so well. As odd as it may sound, before he ever falls in love with you, you will have to first fall in love with yourself. You will need to know and understand yourself.

This is the way this is all going to begin. To get you where you need to go, we will totally modify the content of your life, and you will be the star. We will recognize, portray and embrace the "Personality of You" in Section 3 — and that character will be the star in your life. Furthermore, it's presently not a one-lady show. We will recognize your driving man in Part 2, "The Personality of Him." We will characterize the two characters regarding character, actual attributes, values, convictions and each and every other significant trademark so you know precisely what your identity and you're searching for. You need to know basically everything there is to know about you from the, you need to perceive what your identity is and you need to focus on a "characterized item" of how you will introduce yourself in the social field. The "characterized item " is the most ideal you that is accessible inside the scope of what your identity is, and that is the pony you will ride as far as possible home — right down the walkway. Not any more attempting to be everything to all individuals. Not any more attempting to think about what some man needs and attempting to transform yourself into it. You will be all that you can be, as opposed to someone else, and I guarantee you that will be all that could possibly be needed to make the affection you need.

You will need to identify the aspects of yourself that a man would want. embrace the parts that you don't yet recognize. It ought to be self-evident assuming that you are disrupting yourself. Now that I live in Hollywood, I meet agents everywhere I go. Everybody is trying to get the word out about their undiscovered "star." Imagine if they tried to accomplish that by repeating the same things to themselves about themselves about their future star? Suppose they moved forward and said, "Hello, I got this old stow away of a lady client that I believe you should meet. She's kind of dull and exhausting, doesn't get out a lot and isn't extremely fascinating, at the same time, I don't have the foggiest idea, perhaps you'll like her. She's positively accessible. She hasn't had a date in so long that her clothes are out of style. When you consider the possibility of someone describing another person in that manner, I'm sure that sounds pretty absurd. Assuming this is the case, for what reason doesn't it sound ludicrous to you when you depict yourself that way?

You won't prevail in the profoundly aggressive dating game except if you are persuaded that you are totally awesome.
When you obtain the abilities and capacities important to play the dating game and play it effectively, results will come.

So I'm letting you know that your concern finding the right person doesn't have anything to do with your own value or worth. It isn't so much as an issue of shallow things like your engaging quality. It is, be that as it may, an issue, established in the thing you are doing and not doing. That presumably seems like the terrible news. However, I believe it is simply additional good news given that you can alter your behavior. We are going to assist you with doing that. We're going to tackle your concern, and it won't include a season pass to the plastic specialist or the psychologist. You can meet that one person who is just right for you. You can start a relationship that will satisfy all of your desires and help you realize your childhood ambitions. I'm absolutely serious. If you agree with the ideas I'm about to lay out, do the things I'm going to tell you to do, and use the methods we'll come up with together: solved the issue! It doesn't matter if you can't get a date or the right date, or if you can't get the man in your life to ask you out, or if the man you married doesn't show his love and respect for you. You and I will change all that — and also, we will have an outright ball making it happen. Now is the right time to get what you need!

I don't believe you should frenzy, and I surely don't maintain that you should feel like you've proactively missed the transport, yet the time has come to quit consuming sunlight and to perceive that this is no dress practice. This is Kickoff. Consider this: You're simply going to carry on with a sum of around 25,000 days and no more. That is only 3,900 weeks! Assuming you're in your thirties, you've just got around 12,000 days — 1,800 weeks — left, or 1,800 ends of the week to go to your feline and say, "We should look at what's on Creature Planet." Did you get that? You can gauge what's left of your life in weeks! Weeks! Truly, life can and will travel every which way in a rush. Now is the ideal time to begin playing the game to dominate, and that implies that you need to plan. I've often said that winners do things that losers don't want to do is what separates winners from losers. Now is the ideal time to carry on like a champ.

Here is a primary concern truth: Dating as far as you might be concerned is basically one of the most wasteful, useless, erratic and a mix of good and bad ways of attempting and accomplish one of the main goals of your whole life. When it's all said and done, offer me a reprieve, how weak is regular date manner of speaking: " So what's your sign? Can you believe how much rain we've had? This week, did you read People magazine? Louise, oh my! Before the appetizers arrived, I would be looking for a rope to hang myself from. It's a marvel we haven't vanished as an animal types, inferable from a closure of reproduction. In the event that you go into the dating field, as a great many people, with no preparation, no understanding, no arrangement and no methodology, you're similar to a rocket without a direction framework. You are comparable to a vehicle without a steering wheel. You're just driving around in the hope that Mr. Right will get on the hood, knock on your windshield, and yell, "Hey, stop! It's me, it's me, you tracked down me!" Based on how you've probably been playing the game thus far, I think you'd just hit the wipers and washers to get rid of him like a bug. It's possible that you've already hit him twice! Assuming that is the situation, hopefully he's not a legal counselor!)

I want us to take action, just like the vulture sitting up on a telephone line and telling the other vulture, "Forget this waiting." I'm going to kill something right now. That is how I want you to be. I need you out there getting things going. That's what to do, you really want to have an unmistakable system and you want to have the right stuff to execute that procedure. From getting seen the entire way to finalizing the negotiation. Section 9, "Infrared Dating," will tell you the best way to get to the point with possible accomplices so you're not staying there arranging Harden 0 confines for quite a long time a relationship that never had a future, never got an opportunity to inhale on its own past a couple of irregular great times. In Chapter 7, "Your Man Plan," I'm going to talk to you about where to go to meet potential partners—at a nightclub, gym, church, or online—to find out who is real and who is a waste of time and how to behave when you get there. We'll talk about online dating in Chapter 8, "Fishing with a Net."

Effective dating, on the other hand, is difficult. I can't help thinking about how people at any point get together regardless, not to mention stay together. There couldn't be two more unique "species" on the substance of the planet. I can recollect that when I was youthful, I thought all felines were young ladies and all canines were young men, and that is the reason they didn't get along. After some time, I was able to get that straightened out, but I have to admit that after all these years have passed, I have come to the conclusion that I might have been much closer to the truth when I was five!

A career psychologist like my father used to say that men didn't know anything about women. The day I wedded Robin, he snickered and said there were twice in any man's life that he will be confounded by ladies: before he gets hitched and after he gets hitched. I got the impression that he had not learned this from a book, but rather from difficult life experiences!

Although men and women may not understand each other as well as we would like, I do understand how men think because I am a man. I mean to be like your "companion at the production line." In Section 6, "Your Person Q," we sort out some way to get men to do what you maintain that they should do and not do what you don't believe they should do. My insight is experiential in that I am a man and it's observational in that I have invested a great deal an energy around a ton of folks, some of them dog canines, some of them not. But you need to know what makes a man tick, why he might be afraid of commitment, what he wants, and what it will take for him to see the value in you. If you want to adopt a new last name or hyphenate one you already have, you will need to understand men.

I will zero in not on recondite contrasts, but rather on the things that truly make a difference to you in your mission to track down a man to impart your life to, for example, how to get men to focus on marriage, how to conquer their obvious apprehension about responsibility and how to best guarantee that they esteem you as a lady and treat you with pride and regard.

This will not be an easy deal because men and women have very different priorities, particularly when it comes to starting a committed relationship and getting married. Consider it. Young ladies grow up playing spruce up and having dream weddings. They grow up planning a wedding, acting it out, and covering their heads with towels to look like veils. What do you think men do? We've all heard of the little girls who marry their brothers' G.I. Joes by marching their Barbies down "the aisle." However, have you ever heard of a young boy who broke into his sister's house and stole her Barbie so that she could marry his lonely G.I. Joe? Have you at any point seen a young man destroy tissue paper and put it on a doll's head, imagining that it is a cloak?

When there is such a disparity in priorities, then, what should you do? The response is that you need to make inspiration in your man; you need to make a feeling of want and direness. Similarly as with a great deal of different things, doing that is simple when you know how and it's like attempting to get water to run uphill when you don't. A ton of men have let me know throughout the long term that with regards to dating or being seeing someone, feel they are being pursued, followed and focused on to become spouses. This is somewhat perturbing. You know how ladies generally say that men are keen on just something single. I can assure you that men have their own version of that tale; men believe that you, too, are only interested in one thing. The objective is to make a need to get moving without the impression of tension. I suppose there is some symmetry there because men and women both believe there is a clear cause-and-effect relationship between what they want! And keeping in mind that marriage may as a matter of fact be your essential goal, you super aren't that a very remarkable danger to a man who thinks he esteems his "opportunity" — in light of the fact that, to be perfectly honest, I think most ladies just aren't truly adept at finalizing the negotiation. Face the facts: It is time to rectify the situation if you lack technique. I will show you how in Part 10, "Pack them, Tag them, Bring them back Home." On the off chance that you will make a genuine association with a man, trap him, yet catch his heart, brain and soul AND make him like requiring some serious expertise — you're going. Desperation without pressure is the objective. Explicitly you really want to know how to track down the perfect man, draw in him, persuade him and wed him. That is gruff, however if that is the thing you need to realize that is the thing we will do and live it up while we're making it happen.

In the event that you're as of now hitched to a man, and you simply need to re-get those fires going and keep them consuming, you also will require the serious expertise from Part 11, "The Province of Your Association."

This book isn't tied in with tracking down Mr. Perfect At this point; it is tied in with tracking down Mr. Perfect. I say that since a tremendous contrast between is having the option to get a man to say "I do" at a given second in time and having the option to get him (or you) to say, "I'm joyfully hitched as long as possible." On the off chance that you want to get to "I do," you have an alternate arrangement of guidelines from what you have on the off chance that your objective is "I'm." To get to "I do" you simply let a man know anything he desires to hear just to inspire him to say those words and stroll down the path. You can then zero in on the significant issues of contending with your mother about food providers and photographic artists. Yet, you won't be cheerfully hitched. Indeed, you'll get your fantasy day, however you will miss the mark concerning a fantasy life. On the off chance that you're searching for over an extended period of wedding arranging, an extravagant dress and a major party; on the off chance that what you need is a strong relationship in view of a groundwork of adoration and mindful; If what you want is more than just an "I do," but rather a sincere and resolute "I am happily married," then closing the deal is not about finding any man but rather about developing a relationship with the right man that will benefit you both. Presently how about we get everything rolling.

CHARACTER ASSESMENT

The signs are everywhere: Your natural clock is ticking boisterously to the point that your neighbors can hear it; your stomach presumably turns at the possibility of going to another noisy, smoke-filled bar just so a lot of folks can stare at you like a twenty-ounce porterhouse (with a heated potato as an afterthought); also, you're believing, "In the event that I need to continue even another date with another hair-gelled, shades around evening time wearing nice guy who spends more on garments than I do, I will hurl in my mouth." Assuming that is you and you need off the dating circuit, it is the ideal opportunity for you to quit behaving like a position novice, only looking and hanging tight for an irregular person to pick you. In the event that you will adore shrewd, you must date savvy. You've that is old news — it's the ideal opportunity for the following period of your life to start.

Then again, you might be the sort who never goes on dates or to clubs. You're an untouchable who couldn't actually sort out some way to get into the game to the point of being tired of it, significantly less the way in which you'll at any point find the person you need. You've watched Sex and the City and believed it's a fantasy — "No chance are there ladies out there who are dating as much as these four," not when your last date was the point at which the macarena beat out all competitors! I'm with you there. Like such a large amount what you see on TV or on the big screen, that show and others as it mirror no world I've known about. To that end such countless individuals watch them, wishing life truly could be like that. Perhaps you're like that. Perhaps you've lived vicariously through each celebrity and lighthearted film you can imagine and you've had it up to your ragged looking eyeballs with watching the world go by.

Whether you're a "no need to relive that" lady or an "I don't actually have the foggiest idea how to arrive" lady doesn't exactly make any difference much. The two sorts of ladies are in almost the same situation. Whichever you will be, you haven't had the option to get a traction on a quality relationship with a quality person. Furthermore, that isn't on the grounds that you're a failure, but since you haven't exactly gone at this like a victor — with the arrangement and range of abilities important to boost your possibilities.

Men ought to be like Kleenex — delicate, solid and expendable.

Therefore, here we are. We should get down to what's really going on with this part — composing a person profile of "him." Who precisely, definitively, explicitly do you view as a quality person? Sorting this out now doesn't imply that you ought not be liquid and open to change, yet it serves to essentially begin considering some goal. I won't attempt to transform you into some high-upkeep, hyperpicky downer. I simply need to assist you with halting kissing frogs and begin tracking down your man. Here is where we set a few norms and begin figuring out how to dismiss those folks who fall such a long ways underneath the bar that they do right by prisoners. This is tied in with starting in view of the end (as Dr. Stephen Flock would agree) and not messing with a dog canine when what you truly need is somebody with a family — or in any event, somebody who's housebroken and will not chew on the furnishings!

Furthermore, kid, are there a great deal of dog canines out there. A lady was letting me know as of late about this person who was coming on major areas of strength for super attempting to deeply inspire her at a retreat in Aspen, Colorado. James Bond, in comparison, was modest when he heard her tell his story. She said in the event that he'd been any more brimming with himself, she would have needed to get a table for three rather than two just so his self image wouldn't need to stand.
It appeared that he was regaling her with tales of all the status symbols that he cherished as his own: his Porsche stopped out front; his new Reach Wanderer, which was being hand-waxed back at his carport; his gold Rolex, which he kept on flashing in case she missed it. He talked about his Prada shoes and his craft assortment. No disgrace — his tall structure apartment suite, his boat in the marina, he forgot about nothing. The person had no disgrace — like a server glad for himself for having impeccably discussed the specials he wrapped it up with a priggish look that appeared to say, "So what is your take?" She looked at him dead without flinching and expressed, "Need to understand my

thought process? I think you have a great deal of bills, Smooth. You either possess more cash than brainpower or you are in hawk up to your eyeballs." Absolutely unmoved, she had been staying there the entire time pondering, "What's going on with young men and their toys! I would never, ever spend money on that junk! Jeez, what might be said about a school reserve for my kids, a retirement record, investment funds and a spouse who spends more on his family than his golf clubs? That is my wish!" See, I comprehend the allure of the dog canine. I've already heard that old boys' song and dance numerous times. You must comprehend: It's not always the characteristics of a man that make him a good long-term partner that initially draw you to him. Assuming you are really hoping to settle down you actually don't comprehend that the person pursuing you may not be the individual you need bringing up your kids or being there for you through various challenges, then it's time we get you an arrangement, a profound compass, and begin changing your choice measures right away.

Is there anything wrong with someone who is attractive, supercool, good at dancing, and fun on dates? Definitely not. In point of fact, you might think that those conditions are necessary, and they might be, but that doesn't mean that those characteristics are enough to support what you want.

I don't mean for this to sound like a boring job because, as I mentioned in Chapter 1, this should be an exciting process. But we might as well make sure you're having a good time with guys who have a chance of being "the one" at least. As a result, you should stop spending time with people you absolutely, positively, and positively know will not lead you anywhere. You shouldn't go barhopping because you're afraid of being alone.

In the event that you need what you need when you need it and what you need is a genuine, no doubt about it, quality accomplice and when you need it is presently (or yesterday before early afternoon) rather than a long time from now or never, then you would rather not befuddle capricious social movement with social efficiency.

Here is a demeanor change for you: Conclude right now that you would prefer to be content alone than hopeless with another person. Conclude that you won't pick some person out of dread that you may not get a superior decision later. For instance, unless you're writing a country song, you won't benefit from a guy you know who drinks excessively, has a difficult personality, and despises children. He might be a good time for the evening, yet there's no possibility for a future since he has bargain breaking qualities or values. Even if it means going home alone, you need to pay attention to those and knock on the door.

I know Debbie, a 34-year-old woman who was dating a guy she was insanely attracted to. We're talking catnip. That is to say, she could and did effectively go through hours simply gazing at his image and staring off into space about how provocative he was. However, regardless of all that mooning, she kept a piece of herself down and never let herself get excessively connected. She kept her equilibrium by seeing others since she had been scorched by enchanting "nice guys" previously and realize that once the physical allure settled down, she would be left with an attractive and beguiling person who was likewise incredibly youthful, controlling, reserved and untrustworthy. Sat around! He was only an interruption, taking important time that might have been gainfully enjoyed with genuine conceivable outcomes. She left him a long ways behind.

On the off chance that you haven't halted to give your necessities and needs some serious idea, you presumably wouldn't know Mr. Perfect on the off chance that he approached you wearing an ID. You don't fit with everyone, and not every person fits with you. There are individuals out there who will make you insane as well as the other way around. I need to ensure that you have a reasonable vision of what you need and what you don't need — what you totally can't live with versus "Indeed, this is the establishment on which I can fabricate a future."

A hint for you: What you need isn't be guaranteed to Brad Pitt, George Clooney, Gandhi and Bill Doors generally moved into one. All things considered, as he progresses in years, he's probably going to have Bill Doors' looks and Gandhi's cash. You're not going for some fantasy fellow here, in light of the fact that going for a fantasy fellow is an effective method for pardoning yourself from the game — just set the bar so high that no one estimates up, then, at that point, shrug your shoulders and say, "That is the reason I'm distant from everyone else." No, we are going to enter the room and be realistic in order to locate someone who might be the right kind of guy. Then we'll make the right sort of involvement.

101 Deal Breakers: When describing his character, it's just as important to say what you don't want as what you do want. Thus, first we should make a fast rundown of what you don't

need and totally won't endure. These are what I call issues. They are the attributes, characteristics and qualities that conflict with your basic beliefs: that arrangement of standards and convictions — like genuineness, equity and fortitude — which you use to pass judgment on character and moral fiber and which effectively keep up with your honesty. In the event that somebody has qualities that obviously opposed this basic belief framework, it doesn't a lot matter how charming you think he is or how decent a vehicle he drives. Assuming there is something about him that you realize will drive you out of your consistently cherishing mind quickly by any means, then you really want to resolve that issue on the spot.

Trust me, assuming that you're managing a person who is broken in some significant manner, advise him to find support, provide him with the name of a decent guide however don't take that on when you actually have a choice to shrewdly pick. Although it may sound harsh, you are seeking a partner who is healthy, functional, and uniquely compatible with you. You are not a shelter, you're not Ms. Fix-It and, in any case, he as of now has a mother! Assuming you are hitched or profoundly infatuated or both and your accomplice has created serious defects and issues, that is something else. You are at an alternate stage. You've promised to show up for him, to help and guide him, to calmly assist him with recuperating what troubles him, however not with the eventual result of being pointless.

Taking on large issues, be that as it may, is simply stupid. Don't think that being a rescuer and earning your place will help you succeed. Consolidating two lives without problems like that is sufficiently intense. You genuinely deserve a completely working, solid, quality mate. You must beginning settling on various decisions, and that implies at this moment: Unless you're starting a rock band, no wounded, crazy, or broken-winged men, alcoholics, or drug addicts are required to apply. No harmful, impolite jerks who are decent one moment and mean the following, and afterward come slithering back in a winding of culpability. These folks are not prone to improve, and on the off chance that they do, it should accompany proficient assistance and not on your life.

The good news is that you don't have to take the guy who violates your core values because there are enough people out there—enough fish in the sea—who don't. It's the clearest rule on the planet: Try not to pick the person who is broken. It resembles purchasing a vehicle. On the off chance that two vehicles are staying there, and one has been destroyed while the other doesn't have a scratch on it, hell, even Lassie knows to pick the one that isn't harmed.

So close to the undeniable issues that we recently talked about, what are your own issues? Assuming you are truly strict and wedding somebody outside your religion is something you can't manage, simply don't go down that walkway. In the event that really focusing on your family and investing energy with them is a major piece of your life, however he likes to invest time alone with you, that is a family fight holding back to detonate. This kind of relationship usually ends in heartbreak. In the event that you are searching for significant eye to eye connection, however he'd prefer gaze at his appearance in the mirror looming over your head, then you might have an egotist on your hands. On the off chance that you distinguish even a smidgen of instability, give careful consideration. Do bar brawls will quite often chase after him? Does he struggle with remaining calm? I've frequently said the best indicator of future way of behaving is significant past way of behaving. So check the person's set of experiences out.

Try not to feel that you are such a powerful female power that you are the person who can tame the monster. In the event that he has been hitched three or multiple times, has had four illicit relationships (that you know about), can't hold a task and is monetarily flippant, then he really wants a sedative firearm, not a sweetheart. He might be adorable and enchanting, yet on the off chance that he beverages, battles and bets, continue to walk. I know that sounds so clear I ought not be throwing away life on it, however we both know individuals, perhaps you, who simply don't appear to be ready to stay away. You can't pick a person whose core values, traits, or characteristics compromise you because there are too many fish in the sea. Once a suitable fish is placed in your boat by us, you are free to gut, clean, and fry it however you please. Obviously, this is a joke, but you will have options!

Presently I've gone through and provided you with a short rundown of issues worth considering, and you might have others. When those are found, they turn into stop signs. Put them on your "launch" list and simply don't go there.

The Experience of You

I believe you should expect briefly that you have found someone
who rings your ringer, gets your fire going and gets your engine
running — all simultaneously. We should simply expect you've
found him and he is absolutely a willing soul. Let me know how
you feel, realizing that this individual is blindly enamored with
you?

Is it safe to say that you are feeling a feeling of having a place? A
feeling of acknowledgment? Is it true that you are feeling
fortunate, honored and pleased with yourself and of your
accomplice? Do you feel harmony, bliss, security? Do you believe
you have at last found your place in this world through this
individual with whom you will share you life?

That is the very thing that you truly need — those sentiments
and not the personality of him are your genuine objective. So for
what reason would we say we are going to go through the most
common way of fostering the Personality of Him? Since those
are the attributes and characteristics prone to make this feeling
we have quite recently depicted. So while you really must have a
list of things to get, it's similarly critical to recollect that you're
truly searching for the person that will give you the inclination.
Also, brace yourself for what I'm about to tell you, when you
discover that inclination, you won't really mind what covering it
comes in.

For example — and I can express this with very nearly 100%
sureness — scarcely any tall ladies grow up longing for wedding

a person who's scarcely sufficiently tall to continue every one of the rides at a carnival or requirements a stepladder to change a light on a work area light. Truth be told, the main thing that the greater part of the single tall ladies I know ask while considering a prearranged meeting is, "How tall would he say he is?" In any case, to the extent that tall wedded ladies go, their spouses arrive in various sizes. Also, accept me, the tall young ladies who wedded short folks aren't lounging around reviling their destiny. A long way from it.

Finding genuine affection is as much about you as your accomplice. Ask yourself: What do you desire? A dearest companion who fulfills you," "Somebody you can't survive without," "An individual with whom you need to share" . . . Notice that there's a great deal of "you" in there since genuine romance, regardless of whether you feel it, depends on you. It truly is a decision.

What's more, I would rather not make this excessively clinical, in light of the fact that I realize there is some science included and lightning strikes what not. I see that. I truly do. However, on the other hand, a lot of it comes from thinking, "You know what? I will sprout where I'm planted. This is where I am, so I will focus on this and I will make it happen."

Furthermore, don't allow yourself to be allured by his attractive features; he needs to cause you to feel the manner in which you need to feel. Actual traits that appear to be so significant at the outset become shallow. Level, weight, hair tone, work and that large number of kinds of things that might have drawn in you to him at first and made your chest expand proudly when you stroll into a party together will be at the lower part of the rundown depicting the Personality of Him. That is on the grounds that what you are searching for is the experience of you and not the Personality of Him. What's more, the things that will make this for you will be his qualities, character style and connection style, and the manner in which he assists you with feeling.

We will distinguish the Personality of Him to give you a few rules. However, whether he's short, tall, calm, unconstrained or easygoing, the main thing is what you feel when you are around him. Is your inclination going to be sufficient? " You respond, "Well, geez, I feel that way with this alcoholic here." You might feel as such now, it might ring your chime today, yet it won't in the long haul, and for that reason you will require the rules we recognize in this section.

Allow me to provide you with a fair warning: On the off chance that you assume you have met Mr. Great, you really want to insult yourself or scrub down, since you are entranced. The 100% up-and-comer doesn't exist. Truth be told; the ideal fit is a fantasy straight up there with effortless dentistry and easy waxing. In the event that you truly accept there's an ideal fit, you're presumably as yet checking your directives for that person you met at a club last year who guaranteed he'd call. Assuming you think you've tracked down the ideal man, don't yell it from the housetops. Return home, settle down and accept it as a sign that people in love don't care about the details and you are messing with yourself.

Everything I'm saying to you is that as opposed to with nothing to do looking for a careful match, search for the person who is liberated from the issues and has 80% of what you truly do need in an accomplice. The other 20% you can develop. Assuming the person has 80% of what you need and potential to develop the additional 20%, you really want to pack that kid up on the grounds that he is all set. Try not to stroll past him while you're searching for Mr. 100%, in light of the fact that another person will wed Mr. 80% and you will be remaining there 60% miserable and 40 percent baffled.

I've guided many couples and I've been companions with many couples and I will let you know that in the entirety of my years as a companion, specialist and person cooperating on the planet, I still can't seem to stumble into the "ideal couple." That ideal couple is a fantasy, so don't burn through your time attempting to turn into the first. Am I advising you to think twice about? Indeed, obviously I'm. Life is a split the difference. Connections are a split the difference. Does that mean you ought to abandon the 20% you could do without? No way. You work on it. What's more, assuming all you at any point get is 80% of that missing 20%, take my statement, you will be hitched and glad for quite a while.

At last it boils down to the contrast between individuals who don't joke around about responsibility and individuals who are out pursuing a dream — the previous will happily neglect the blemishes of a 80 percent accomplice for the present, though the last option will continue to look until they sort out that a 100% match is probably essentially as genuine as 100 dollar Rolex.

Spouses Limitless

Since you're two sections into this book, I figure that you fully intend to take care of business and I need to give you the devices you want to assist you with tracking down your join forces with least experimentation. Champions have a method called perception, by which they really see and feel what it resembles to win before they've even begun the game. You've proactively portrayed what it might feel want to have what you need in the segment of this part headed "The Experience of You." Presently, we will imagine the individual who will cause you to feel that multitude of magnificent, blissful feelings that will accompany being important for a couple.

Envision that we are making a film of your life. Your responsibility is to compose a magnificent content about how you believe your story should unfurl, especially your heartfelt story line. The main thing you'll need to do is depict your driving man, a.k.a. your future spouse. I maintain that you should be very unambiguous while imagining this man. That's what to do, you might have to ponder the sorts of male characters you've found in your life. How about we play some original film jobs similarly as specific illustrations (these are neither genuine individuals nor great "measuring sticks," yet I use them as models since we both know them): Tom Hanks is your delicate dream fellow in Restless in Seattle. He is a closest companion, a dad, a nurturer. He's entertaining and dry — the sort of fellow who can find a place with any gathering. On the opposite finish of the range is Richard Gere in Lovely Lady. He plays serious areas of strength for a magnate — rich, strong and ordering. He is liberal and steady, refined and modern — a man who accompanies a way of life. Then, at that point, you have your enthusiastic and sincerely expressive sort in Screwy: Nicholas Enclosure. This person is the pith of intensity and science. At the point when he needs you, you know it, and neither downpour, nor snow, nor hail nor slush will prevent him from pursuing you. The rundown goes on, yet the characters are totally obvious, and assuming you remember them you realize they had explicit attributes that went a long ways past the short portrayal above.

That is the manner by which exact I maintain that you should be while envisioning your future spouse. You must ponder what you need intellectually, genuinely, inwardly, occupationally, socially, mentally — everything that make you say, "Gee, presently there's a person I wouldn't see any problems with going through my time on earth with." Assuming that you're circumventing saying, "I'll know it when I see it," I have news for you: The main thing you will see is every other person meeting the right person. So we should not squander one more moment. Let's determine the kind of man you want right now.

Go through the accompanying five records and circle all that you can envision as a beneficial quality in your extraordinary somebody. Relax assuming your list of things to get appears to be excessively lengthy. Circle however many things in every class as you want. Ponder you, your life and your likely focuses as you go. Which characteristics could get you all worked up? Which ones will make your life simpler? Furthermore, which ones have you been searching for from the start?
Social style: This is about how you need your fantasy fellow to connect with you. Could it be said that you are keen on someone

who believes you should be his beginning and end and remembers you for every one of the plans he makes? Or on the other hand could you lean toward a different and confidential life and wouldn't fret a different get-away every so often? Do you need a heartfelt who says and does characteristically heartfelt things? Let me tell you, if you marry a man who doesn't have it in him and needs a love letter every week, you could be disappointed for years. The equivalent goes for nurturing styles. Do you prefer a man who will take responsibility for that, or one who will delegate child rearing to you?

What about the topic of money, too? What is Mr. Wonderful's position regarding the significance of finances in a relationship? Does he trust that it's a monetary association, meaning it's "our" cash and we will present on all choices, or does he like to assume the weight of liability regarding the monetary preparation? Do you need a person who needs a pleasant house, a three-vehicle carport, a beefed up sound system, the most recent television, refreshed kitchen machines, the works, or somebody who doesn't take an excess of confidence in material features?

Then, at that point, you have your sexual issues. Do you need somebody who is profoundly charged, or is once a month fine and dandy by you? Are you a traditional or sexual vixen? In this regard, you must know what you want. If you and your partner are sexually compatible, your relationship will have more chemistry, heat, and intensity.

Think about how your ideal man would treat you in a

relationship, and then write down the descriptions that come to mind.

graph Sincerely expressive. Expresses his sentiments.

outline Tender. Shows feeling through much love.

chart Heartfelt in every one of the ways Trademark would anticipate.

diagram Model of active involvement in parenting.

outline In charge of funds.

diagram Willing to share financial responsibility.

diagram Extremely sensual

diagram Not sexual at all.
outline Reserved and doesn't need or offer a lot of consideration.

diagram Compassionate while remaining objective.

chart Cash propelled and a hard worker who should have all the common luxuries.

diagram A solitary bohemian who does not require many creature comforts.

outline Somebody who adamantly requests to get everything he could possibly want.

outline Open to think twice about.

chart Indivisible from you.

outline Needing a great deal of individual space.

outline Profound similarity: Regardless of whether you are strict, the truth of the matter is that ideally you would presumably like your accomplice to concur with your view on this. Or not. Perhaps you'd prefer have a home with different viewpoints. Whatever your situation, once more, it's ideal to understand what you need going in. Profound convictions are profoundly imbued during our childhood, and the opportunity that somebody will go from a prized conviction framework isn't perfect. Positively, individuals are much of the time brought back to life, however in the event that you're a reliable Christian, perhaps you shouldn't wed a skeptic and petition God for a supernatural occurrence until the end of your life. That is the meaning of disappointment.

Investigate the accompanying rundown and verify whichever way to deal with otherworldliness works for you.

chart He is exceptionally perceptive of a similar religion as you.

chart He is to some degree perceptive of a similar religion as you.

outline He isn't the slightest bit perceptive, yet comes from a similar strict foundation as you.

graph He isn't in any way shape or form strict yet has confidence in a higher power.

diagram He has no faith whatsoever in a higher power.

outline It doesn't make any difference what he accepts for however long he is liberal and aware of your convictions.

chart Actual attributes: Presently we should conclude what you'd like Mr. Astonishing to seem to be. Is he required to be a large man? Or on the other hand perhaps you're modest and you need a more modest person? Is it true or not that he is athletic? Does he have to have hair? (Heads up!) Provided that this is true, do you like brown, fair or red hair? Certainly, this might appear to be shallow; also, no doubt, you likely could think, "What difference does it make? so long as he has everything else I want?" It all makes sense to me, yet humor me. It's most certainly not by any means the only thing — it's not so much as something critical — yet it's essential for the equation you get. So go on, fill in or circle what you'd need assuming that you had your druthers.

That was the tomfoolery part. At least on paper, you now have your 80 percent guy. Presently comes the crucial step. Whenever you blend two lives, there is continuously going to be some agony of change. You must forfeit a portion of your time, space, cash, exertion and opportunity — and you surely must think twice about some of what you need.

Now that you're through orbiting your needs, revisit your

decisions and cross off all the extravagance things you can manage without. What's more, I amount to something that can fall into the 20% of the 80-20 equation. What remains is your norm. Even if the guy who fits this description doesn't immediately pique your interest, if you let him get you away from your TiVo, you might just end up having a great time.

Get Serious Now, go over your needs list once more. Is it still excessive? Is everything an unquestionable requirement? Have you ruled out split the difference? Is it safe to say that you are restricting yourself with your elevated expectations? Find opportunity to think about your decisions previously. Or, if you absolutely have to, think about the cell phone that is no longer ringing. What are the issues? On the off chance that your rundown is as long as my arm, I know why no men are calling — you're more elite than the celebrity room at the Vanity Fair Oscar party!

This is an ideal opportunity to put on a few optics and look somewhat more profound into the field of competitors. Let's assume you want a vehicle. You need power situates however you must have cooling. Now, let's say you can't afford either. Is it safe to say that you will use whatever might remain of your days strolling to work or would you say you will manage your rundown? So suppose you meet a person who has the genuineness and the desire. Perhaps you can figure out how to live without the funny bone.

You have the opposite issue if all the wrong men are calling you. You are not being sufficiently selective. Mass promoting can be exceptionally rewarding — in the event that you've thought of an extraordinary new item for putting away extras. However, if you promote your highly sought-after companionship, you might be underselling yourself. You will be overwhelmed with demands and have no savvy method for picking and pick. One young woman I know stays at home about twice a month. I'm not joking with you. She is out constantly, either with her companions or with some person. In any case, one of the makers I work with invests energy with her, and the manner in which she tells it, it's a quite sorry sight. When asked, the girl will go out with anyone. Hell, even drive-through joints don't give everybody access. These two ladies have raised a ruckus around town together, and the maker tells me, "You might have a hard time believing the failure that was hitting on Marisol the previous evening. Be that as it may, get this — she really gave him her number. Her genuine number." The young lady has no channel. Anyone who asks her will go out with her. She's very nearly thirty years of age, however she's still as frantic for consideration as a five-year-old.

So check your rundown out. Is it, truth be told, excessively short? You might have been a bad equal-opportunity dater. Also, perhaps at this point, you're beginning to accept that all men are washouts since you meet such countless unseemly ones. Lady, you need to put some barriers around yourself if you selected less than five characteristics from that wish list. Compared to community colleges, you might be easier to get into. Have a few limits. Learn about your true preferences. And don't just listen to the part of you that can't stand being on your own. Try not to be the young lady who would prefer to have a date, any date, than go through a night with a hot shower and a decent book.

When you do that, you accidentally make yourself alone, or at least in company with the wrong people, which can be very lonely.

Moving on Now that we've talked about what you want in a man and what you know you won't stand, you know who you want. More significant, notwithstanding, you've understood that you can't become amped up for a list of references or a worked out rundown of characteristics. What gets you moving is the possibility of an organization with somebody you regard and need to invest energy with, and the feeling of having a place and satisfaction that this person gives.

Your goal is to have that warm, fuzzy feeling of being a part of a couple. Not a guy who meets all of your requirements and wears the suit. There are a lot of guys who fit the bill, but it takes time to find the guys who help you feel and give you the experience you want. But the search will be much simpler for you now that you know what you want.

SOCIAL LIFE

On the off chance that you're similar to the a large number of ladies I've conversed with, you're likely reasoning there are a great many hot, youthful, single young ladies and every one of the heroes are taken or gay — or perhaps both. You're giving it your best shot to keep up. Cost-effective haircuts? Check. trips to all of the right places to vacation? Twofold check. A gym subscription? Hanging out at the objective rich conditions also called "in vogue dance club" or "new eatery bars"? Check, check, check. Nevertheless, you feel like you're wearing yourself out, running on a treadmill and wasting time quick and perspiring simultaneously. You're lounging around scratching your head and pondering, "What's going on with me? Why her and not me? Is this a type of dog biscuit? For what reason might I at any point appear to get a person to save my life while that young lady who is unkempt, messy, smokes and has five piercings in her lip is strolling connected at the hip with what resembles Jude Regulation's more youthful sibling! or a guy who doesn't look very good but looks pretty cool.

I don't have any idea how to address that particular inquiry, since I don't have any acquaintance with you. It's possible that people see something wrong. Perhaps they think you look, act or smell entertaining, I don't have the foggiest idea, however I'm wagering it's none of those three things. I won't mess with you: It's a cruel dating world out there, and if you have any desire to win and have your desired relationship you must raise your game. Yes, it is, in my opinion, "a game," at least at this level and stage. I know, I know, I can hear some of you with all the progress of Auntie Honey bee saying, "Indeed, Andy, I don't think finding a soul mate to go into the holiness of marriage is any sort of a game. So there." All I can perceive you is that you're not strolling down the passageway right now, so ease up around 1,000 percent and have a great time!

Men and women have been "playing the game" and "doing the dance" for centuries in the highly competitive social market. It doesn't debase the interaction in the event that you play with trustworthiness and are what your identity is. You must first understand who you are and then commit to being that person.

So how are you going to go from remaining uninvolved and watching others score to taking the ball to the circle yourself? How are you going to get off the never-ending dating merry-go-round, where one cool jerk after another can't even commit to a hairstyle, let alone a relationship with you? Truly, what are you going to do — shy of moving to Gold country, joining a brotherhood or finding a new line of work on the floor of the stock trade where the chances are ten to one in support of yourself?

First of all, I'm going to let you know that you probably have it right: It's possible that Carole in accounting isn't any funnier, prettier, or cooler than you. The explanation you've spent the last four Friday evenings staring at the television with your feline while her end of the week evenings are reserved a long time ahead of time is that she is better — better at the game. I've said it multiple times, "It is possible that you get it or you don't." What you really want to get is what's genuinely going on with this section — how to recognize the best-quality Person of You. That implies being straightforward with yourself about your assets and shortcomings, which isn't simple all the time. It very well may be difficult to concede that you may some of the time be timid or controlling, or anything your shortcomings might be, however knowing and tolerating them gives you a certainty that can't be faked. This awareness also enables you to comprehend how those characteristics may, in the short or long term, turn people off and how you can control them to prevent them from interfering with your relationships.

Whenever you've distinguished and embraced all aspects of the Personality of You, you can put whichever qualities you wish out into the world as a characterized item. Take me, for instance. You are aware of what you are getting when you watch the Dr. Phil show, purchase a Dr. Phil book, or attend a Dr. Phil speech because it is a clearly defined product. Being a direct, straightforward, in front of you portrayal of reality is going. That is the characterized item that is Dr. Phil. In any case, that is definitely not a full portrayal of my Personality of You. There is so much more, like my husbandism, fatherhood, and involvement in my church community; what I for one accept and esteem; You don't get to see everything in my life story every time. Yet, anything specific setting you experience me in, what you really do get to see is a genuine subset of my Personality of You. It's real, it's me, and it's true, but what I choose to say is appropriate for that circumstance.

The Personality of You is the wide and comprehensive meaning of who you are from the back to front, while the characterized item is anything side you decide to show in a given social circumstance. Presently beyond a shadow of a doubt: After you've concluded that this is the pony you will ride through the race called life, your whole involvement with the social, dating and making a-relationship field will change for eternity.

In the event that You Couldn't Date You, Who Might?

I'll say it again because it's important to say: The principal individual you need to offer yourself to is you. That is the significant initial step to distinguishing the Personality of You. I call it characterizing your own reality — it's what you tell yourself when no other person is looking. Assuming you're let everybody know that you're the best thing since the iPod, however where it counts inside you accept you are an eight-track player or the "rotund young lady" who couldn't get a man with a net and a pack of hunting canines, then you're setting out toward additional evenings alone than a sheltered religious recluse. You will produce the outcomes that compare to your own reality.

I mean that. I don't care how well-crafted your argument or presentation are; in the event that you have a messy individual truth, you can seem to be Miss Universe as far as I might be concerned. If deep down, you accept you're carrying on with a major untruth since you're simply a loathsome outcast who is bound to meander the planet alone, individuals will detect it instantly and run the alternate way. They will figure, "Hello, she understands herself better than any other person, and in the event that she believes she's useless, why should I contend? See ya!" Or on the other hand perhaps you'll discover some failure who doesn't mind who he's with or what your identity is, just inasmuch as he has someone — anyone. That is not the very thing you need by the same token. You merit better. Trust me when I say that being with someone is very different from being with just one person. You are destined to end up with the leftovers if you are out there acting as though you will take whatever you can get because "beggars can't be choosers."

At the point when your own reality is negative and loaded with questions, bends and disgrace, you shout that message to the world in a great many nonverbal ways. What you accept is your "genuine article" reflects itself in your non-verbal communication, your looks and your activities, which all scheme to go against each word you say and the impression you endeavor to make.

Goodness, I get everything right. You have a set of experiences that perhaps you're not pleased with. Perhaps you've laid down with an adequate number of folks to make up two football crews — including the training crews. You might have been left standing at the altar or dumped. The fact of the matter is that everything is before and you can do nothing to change it. You can begin focusing 5% of your time on determining whether you made a mistake or received a poor deal, and 95% of your time on determining what you will do about it.

Presently, it's conceivable that you have some profoundly dug in scarring in your life like attack or misuse. Assuming these things have happened to you, your enduring is genuine and reasonable. A harmed mental self view, compromised self-esteem and negative self-truth are all not out of the ordinary. Try not to briefly downplay those encounters by letting yourself know that you must destroy up and deal with it. Those encounters can make you degrade yourself. They can prompt many years of accepting that you are harmed products who nobody would need under any circumstance other than sexual delight. While it is off-base reasoning, it is justifiable. You will most likely need to get proficient assistance to conquer that — and not on the grounds that you want it, but since you merit it. Regardless of whether you at any point structure a relationship with another person, the main relationship you will at any point have is the one with yourself. Therefore, seek assistance, if not for the sake of establishing a happy relationship, then for the sake of establishing your own happiness and peace in this life.

Getting your own reality fixed is the initial step to recognizing the Personality of You. Everything about your message, your aura, and who you are will change. If you are unsure of what constitutes your personal truth, the time has come to confront your doubts head-on:

1. Do I feel that I need to mask myself?

2. Do I live with disgrace?

3. Do I carry around guilt?
4. Do I think I'm not smart enough?

5. Is there really something wrong with me?

6. Do I need certainty?

7. Do I think my _____ (dearest companion, sister, and so forth.) is some way or another better than I'm?

8. Do I think I'm being conned?

9. Do I believe that I am a third-class citizen?

10. Do I feel shameful of adoration?

11. Do I frequently feel I have zero power over my life and conduct?

12. Am I harmed products — have I been unloaded so often that there must be some kind of problem with me?

13. Do I think I'm less interesting, smart, or sharp than other people?

14. Do I think I will never find contentment?

15. Do I share with myself that I'm not commendable?

16. Do I feel that I am disguising and only out in front of being found out?

17. Do I think that compared to my peers, I am completely clueless?

18. Do I constantly play the game out of fear of being humiliated and hurt?

I have recently taken you through an organized assessment of conceivable pessimistic substance in your own reality. The primary thing that ought to go on your plan for the day is to take out, recuperate, change, do anything that you need to do so it no longer affects you. Ideally, the majority or even most of your own truth is positive. Most of individuals have a combo bargain.

We all produce the outcomes we believe we deserve, which is why we are conducting this personal truth inventory. So on the off chance that you can dispose of, limit and deal with the negatives, you will actually want to amplify the up-sides and present the outcomes that are reliable with somebody who has positive self-esteem. To put it another way, if you don't like yourself, no one else will either. Others will love you if you love yourself. On the off chance that you accept that you merit the best relationship, you will draw in a sound, positive, satisfying relationship into your life.

Saying, "I am a quality person, so I should be treated in a quality manner" is your personal truth. So when some jerk rolls up, slaps you on the butt and says, "Hello, child, you need to take a tumble?" you can say, "Stand by a moment. Jerk, you don't talk to me that way. I merit preferred treatment over that. You address me as a woman with nobility and regard or you don't address me by any stretch of the imagination." However, on the off chance that you are staying there thinking, "Wow, I will take what I get on the grounds that no one needs me," and someone slaps you on the butt, you might think, "All things considered, essentially I'm getting grabbed and it's better compared to being distant from everyone else." Then, at that point, you're getting what you anticipate. You ought to be telling yourself, "I merit someone to invest energy with me, share encounters with me and get to know me. Not get my butt." Assuming that your own reality is negative, you will make due with being grabbed. Assuming that it is positive, you will not.

To that end I don't need the negative voices in your mind shouting stronger than the positive voices. In the event that any of the responses to the above questions is indeed, focus in and plan to accomplish some genuine work. You will need to transform each of those self-destructive responses and the perceptions that led you to them into positive, constructive thoughts if you want to truly sell yourself on yourself. Whenever you have sold yourself on you, you'll understand that you needn't bother with a man in that frame of mind to be entirety. What's more, that is getting your head in the game — coming at it with the mentality of a champ, not a washout. Since, in such a case that you're letting yourself know that you would do well to find an accomplice quick or you'll simply twist up and pass on, then you are playing with sweat-soaked palms, behaving irrationally, falling off frantic and switching folks off — and folks sense distress the manner in which a canine detects a seismic tremor; also, when they do, they take off and never think back. You've been doing fine on your own such an extremely long time, so only let it all out. It's not so alarming to go out and show the world what your identity is.

The Personality of You Passing on to Get Out

Who are you? Try not to simply overlook this inquiry. This part is basic to characterizing the Personality of You, so view it in a serious way. Give it some serious thought, and then tell me who you are. Presently record it on paper

In the event that you said an educator, an understudy, a little girl and sister, a Christian or a solitary white female, attempt once more. What are you?

I'm _____, isn't that annoying? Who are you?" is an inquiry that prompts another inquiry: " Your meaning could be a little clearer." Do you need my name? My age? My religion? My orientation? My profession? My part in my loved ones? Who I'm with my companions? The individual I am with my business partners? So many of us loathe this inquiry. We could do without expounding on ourselves, or discussing ourselves. We could do without pondering ourselves so much. And if you want to connect with someone in love, that presents a significant challenge.

Getting seen in the singles scene is tied in with reaching out to your own extraordinary person. That is your authority, and nothing else will suffice. You need to know what your identity is and disregard all the other things. At the point when I do interviews, now and again radiated through satellite to stations all around the country, I can end up conversing with many broadcasters over the course of about one day. It sometimes feels like you keep talking to the same person. Without a doubt, they have various names and come from various states, however they each have a similar bought grin, a similar perfect hair and a similar Rhonda Radio from No place USA voice. No articulation, no uniqueness, no peculiarity. The ones I recollect, the ones who truly stick out, are the ones who have a little disposition, the hot ones who are individuals first and anchors second. Also, it isn't so much that they're sullen or unpleasant, it's simply that they're not frantically attempting to eradicate their uniqueness to fit focal projecting's "columnist form."

You must be particular like this. You would rather not be any old face in the group. When the tall, thin blondes enter the room, you might think everyone is looking at them, but don't they all kind of look the same? Be somebody unmistakable. I'm not saying you ought to attempt to interest everyone. It's basically impossible that you are out there attempting to get everyone in your postal district to date you. That's simple, and the girl who does it is also simple, which is about as nice of a compliment as you can give her. We as a whole understand what we call that young lady. You are simply attempting to find that one person who has the Personality of Him that fits with the Personality of You.

Some of you are the Jennifer Aniston type: darlings with an appeal and attraction you can't resist the urge to cherish. Then, at that point, you have your Angelina Jolie hottie types. Both women have a lot of success, are very attractive, and would be attractive to a lot of men—even the same man. be that as it may, these ladies are all around as various as constantly. Because they are so different from one another, they stick out. Make an impression, that's what you have to do. Fortunately, there are a variety of ways of doing this that don't include dating Brad Pitt.

There are many ways to excel, but one surefire way to be a

chump is to disappear into the background. The most exceedingly terrible thing that can happen is that you hit up a party or a get-together and the following day, a gathering of folks who were there are talking and not one of them could select you from a setup! In the event that not one of them can recall whether you were the tall young lady or the fair young lady or the young lady with the talking parrot on her shoulder just on the grounds that you neglected to have an effect of any kind, then welcome to Singleville, populace: You!

You maintain that every last one of those folks should have an exceptionally clear and particular memory of you. One might have preferred you and one more might not have really focused on you by any means, however — generally significant the two of them saw you and have no issue reviewing you and their experience of you. How would you get that this done like clockwork? Answer: You distinguish your special Person of You and structure a characterized item that you show the world. Focus on it, amplify it, embrace it and love it. That is the pony that you will ride. Certain individuals will like it and some will not, yet in the event that it is extraordinarily you and you focus on it, you will get another person to focus on it too.

This all beginnings by you tolerating that you are what your identity is. In any case, that doesn't mean you shouldn't work on yourself where and when you can. This isn't a reason to be lethargic. Assuming you are overweight, raise it and get the additional pounds off — for your appearance, however for your wellbeing, energy, confidence and general mentality. Superficial? Perhaps, yet to win, you must work at it and take your game to a higher level. Winners do things that losers do not want to do, which is the difference between winners and losers.

Change your hair and clothes if they make you look like I Love the 80s! You don't maintain that individuals should see you and think, "Goodness, no doubt. I can recall a time when that was fashionable! Glance around, have some friendly responsiveness and get it together. Try not to let yourself know that it's alright and that it shouldn't make any difference in the event that it's not OK. It makes a difference. Change a quality if it can be changed and is worth changing! A five-year-old realizes you ought to transform it. With respect to those characteristics you can't change, similar to your level, your overall insight, your childhood and your experience, now is the right time to acknowledge it and don't think back.

Your Characterized Item

In this part, we will start further developing your game so at some point, somebody can see you strolling with your sweetheart or spouse and say, "What does she have that I haven't got — I mean, other than that extraordinary person on her arm?" At the point when that occurs, you can simply grin and give her your canine eared duplicate of this book.

I'm wagering that those young ladies you're "abhorring," the ones with the truly fair sweethearts, the ones you will resemble when we're through, either got stupid fortunate being perfectly positioned brilliantly or truly had something that you simply don't have. That something is the very thing I call a characterized item and a system for displaying it to the world. Ladies who get what they need throughout everyday life and love have sorted out their own best and most impressive mix of qualities, ways of behaving, actual properties and character attributes that separates them particularly from the wide range of various ladies on the planet. They've transformed these into their characterized item — and afterward they've worked it for everything it has.

Imagine a choir of beautiful voices that are all great but are all the same. Then a soloist moves forward and that voice transcends the rest with celestial tones. That is the very thing we have to do with you. You need to transcend the commotion. You need to turn into the figure against the backdrop of the world. You need to contrast the foundation. What's more, to do that, we should recognize the attributes that put you aside from the ladies around you and make you the soloist in the ensemble of your life.

Presently you might think, "Oh rapture, we've hit an obstacle here since I'm simply not excessively exceptional. I simply don't have those novel attributes and qualities." That is the reason I'm here — to let you know that this isn't correct. You may not see the value in your best characteristics this moment, yet we will find them before we happen to the following two parts. In all actuality, the outcome may not be what you had expected. It may not be all that you would arrange up and plug into yourself assuming you were going down a cafeteria line — "I'll take one request for that sparkly hair and an aiding of charm, please; what's more, many thanks!" You're not Ms. Potato Head, you can't stick on another nose, ears and a mouth, and the individuals who attempt wind up looking more phony than a

Halloween veil — and typically a ton more frightening. In any case, I guarantee you will find that what you really do have truly deserve being adored and really focused on by someone that you love and care about. You can't keep on being the trick of the trade in your life.

Men are not dating criminal investigators. They typically do not actively seek a life partner with the same level of vigor as women. They won't come into your existence with the sole reason for surveying whether you are "the one." They won't dig and pull around searching for the attributes, characteristics and qualities that are the best fit for their extraordinary somebody. They may not understand what those attributes, characteristics and qualities are. Men will invest unending energy exploring another vehicle or a boat or which extra large television has the best picture, yet they simply don't have that relationship-marriage "chip" in their mind at similar level ladies do, which we will discuss in Part 6. That implies you must certainly stand out enough to be noticed. The answer is not to tell them what they think they want to hear. Attempting to think about what they assume they need and fill that bill isn't the response. As you are going to find out, you are not ideal for everyone. In any case, you, and not certain individuals satisfying adaptation of you, will be ideal for someone.

I can assure you that one of the main reasons why some people find the partner they're looking for and others don't is that they have accepted their Character of You and defined that character's product. This unmistakable and particular item made someone be drawn to them. Because it was real, it was powerful; it was bona fide, and it was acknowledged by them well before they chose to attempt to get it acknowledged by "him."

Everyone, including you, has a specific heavenly body of qualities and qualities that, once recognized and showed, makes a power you can't start to envision. As I stated, I don't want you to remain your life's best-kept secret. I don't need you hanging tight for "random karma." I believe that you should make your own karma.

Robin, my wife, is, in my opinion, a perfect example. I will concede that, to some extent as I would see it, she has a major upside that a many individuals don't have. She has always been a "ten" who runs smoothly. Also, I just own it was her looks that definitely stood out enough to be noticed from minute one, however when I met her and began conversing with her, I was hypnotized. She had a sort of guaranteed demeanor: " I'm who I'm, I understand what I need and in the event that you could do without it, another person will." (I actually think she was somewhat feigning and was insane in affection with me, yet she won't ever 'fess up!) She was feisty, flippant and a positive conundrum. She was not a "bad girl," and she certainly wasn't Goody Two Shoes. She was fun, unpredictable, and had a great spirit of adventure, but she was a spunky, "double dog dare ya" kind of girl. She was unquestionably "Woohoo!" when it was time to let loose. She had a powerful and enticing connection when it was time to be quiet. Never, ever monotonous. That was her trademark item. Because it felt real at the time and hasn't changed a whit more than thirty years later, I know it was real. It distinguishes her from others. She couldn't have cared less assuming she had cosmetics on or whether her hair was flawlessly prepped or standing out in 24 headings — she was generally a similar shimmering, energetic Robin. You knew when you were with her you could never be exhausted. In no time, I was endeavoring to win her endorsement, a great spot for her to be in. I need precisely that for you.

I believe that you should be in the power position in your connections so you are the one sought after, as opposed to the follower. Also, trust me, that is the very thing you want to go for. You don't want him anyway, even if you have to chase him down like a hungry cheetah after a gazelle. Connections are intense enough when the two individuals are running toward one another; He won't let go of you if you're in a relationship where he's nervous. You want to catch his eye, show him who you can be in his life, and then let him be "Cheetah Boy." Therefore, you require an advantage. Like that, when you find the unique fellow and he finds you, he will ponder where you have been for his entire life.

You are all familiar with girls who can simply enter a room and rule it. They might not be the most beautiful people in the crowd, they might not fit the media's idea of what it means to be conventionally attractive, and they probably don't even have the most skin, but they always seem to get all the attention. Love them or disdain them. In any case, here's the key part: Certainty and self-acknowledgment are making them so brilliant, and those come just whenever you've dominated the principal rule of the game, which additionally is the main rule of deals: In the event that you're not sold on your item, you will not have the option to sell any other person on it by the same token.

You need to get right with you first. Furthermore, I don't mean simply letting yourself know a lot of rah positive reasoning. I mean truly finding your best credits, your most helpful attributes, the genuine qualities that make you unmistakable. If you're sitting there and saying things like, "Look, I know a funny girl or a good-looking girl when I see one, and I ain't it," you're not being honest. That is not a problem. That should not be the Personality of You and that is fine. I can assure you that whatever you are and whatever you have going for you are plenty good enough if you fully embrace them and show them to the world.

Most of us can distinguish ourselves. Consider me. Every day is a "bad hair day" for me! In any case, so what? How many Hollywood celebrities have you observed and wondered, "How in the world did that person ever become famous?" A valid example: DeVito, Danny The man is scarcely five feet tall, overweight and bare. In the event that you are finishing up list of references for driving men, I don't figure you will see those attributes on the short rundown. However he is a big name. Why? (1) He is talented, 2) He is likeable, and 3) He is different from everyone else in a very big way.

We wouldn't have been able to appreciate Danny's screen presence if he had sat back and said, "I have a face and body for radio." instead of participating.

"Better believe it, however he's a person," you say. " Guys have different experiences, right? Now, just take a look at someone like Kathy Bates. She may not be customarily Hollywood or extraordinarily appealing, yet she is such a charming and strong individual that you can't take your eyes off her! She is multifaceted, adorable, and funny. So don't undercut yourself since you don't satisfy the run of the mill guideline. You don't need to quantify yourself by conventional, normal principles of what makes an individual appealing and engaging.

I Have Versus What He Needs this

The normal grumbling I hear from men is that they're dating Stepford ladies. All they hear when they go out on a date is, "Oh, yes, I completely agree." At first, that seems great. Is there any good reason why you wouldn't adore somebody who prefers every one of your thoughts, giggles at every one of your jokes, centers exclusively around you and becomes involved with all that you say? However, one log won't consume.

I will tell you about something that's usually kept under wraps: men need to feel that they have worked for and acquired something, or they won't esteem it. Come and go with ease. You won't keep his attention if you give up too quickly. From the outset, being pleasing is fine and dandy, yet ultimately we need to know your real assessment, and in the event that you don't have one, you are nap city. A man might get the same thrill from picking up a coma patient as he does from you. Men only want an honest opinion. A man is content regardless of the viewpoint's divergence or even its shocking nature—as long as it is genuine, unflinching, and does not involve human sacrifice, he is content. He enjoys himself. He is curious. He is interested. He thinks he's getting to know you better.

Appears to be basic, however the truth of the matter is that an enormous level of ladies would sooner shave their heads and join the Krishnas than offer a fair viewpoint and risked switching off their date. You might be shaking your head and thinking, "Oh no, that couldn't possibly apply to me." Some of you might be doing that. All things considered, I wouldn't wager on that. Women have been conditioned to look for signs of interest from men before beginning to evaluate their own feelings because men have traditionally been the ones on the lookout. It's the old mentality: I'll expert the meeting, land the position, then, at that point, choose whether to take it" — extraordinary in business, horrible in dating. As a matter of fact, this is unequivocally the mentality that leads so many to betray dating through and through on the grounds that they can't confront the possibility of another "new employee screening" date.

Attempting to be everything to all individuals is at the base of these dull dates and shallow discussions, and it is the single greatest misstep ladies make when they are dating.

Those of you actually staying here thinking, "Indeed, consider the possibility that I simply have no extraordinary attributes." are also held accountable. Permit me to put it this way: What is awesome of what you have? I'm not saying that in the event that you had your druthers, you'd choose those characteristics from a list, yet moderately talking, given just what you need to work with, what are your long suits? Consider it in this way: On the off chance that we were lost in a woods and needed to get by, the primary thing I could ask is, What do we have? Do we have covers, a compass, flares, matches, food, a tent? On the off chance that I'm out there and I don't have a tent, I will pull branches off trees and cover myself up so I don't get frostbite. Of course, I would prefer to have a tent and a Coleman light and a decent open air fire, however I'm living in reality, so I will capitalize on what I have — two arms, two legs and an endurance nature that pushes me to build a stopgap cover.

A few ladies are great at this "utilization what the great master gave you" approach. As of late Robin and I were going to a capability at a lead representative's chateau. We were both going to give a speech in front of a distinguished group of people wearing black tie. Yet, when she opened her bag, she understood that she had brought just a single shoe. Then, at that point, in her scramble to get dressed, she broke one of the spaghetti lashes on her outfit. So we are right here: clock ticking, broken lash on outfit and one shoe. Did she overreact? No. Before I know it, she emerges from the room looking flat out amazing. I have no clue about how she got it done, yet she never thought twice. You ladies know how to make the best of what you have and you do it the entire life. Think back to every time you have done something similar, whether it was fixing that ripped hem with a glue gun or making an entire lunch out of what other people thought was an empty refrigerator. That was all groundwork for what we are referring to here, at this moment. That multitude of encounters were simply setting you up for this second in time.

With regards to characterizing yourself, there is a particular distinction between ladies who say, "This is the very thing I have" and the people who inquire, "What is it that you need?" The first are emphasizing the value they bring to the table. The last option are attempting to characterize themselves as far as their thought process individuals need — a catastrophe waiting to happen in the event that I've heard one.

I'll let you know at the present time, you won't understand what your characterized item is until you've recognized your most grounded ascribes, qualities, resources and attributes. So you want to take a stock and afterward present your discoveries to the world, rather than going around weakly attempting to be everything to all individuals. Constant individuals satisfying either brings an end to the relationship from the outset on the grounds that your potential accomplice detects your thought processes and gets exhausted, or it kills the relationship gradually, after you frustrate every one of the assumptions you've set up. At the point when Robin and I initially began dating, I told her that I play tennis. At the point when I inquired as to whether she played tennis, she said, "Gracious better believe it." So I thought, "Gracious, extraordinary, she looks perfect and a tennis player as well." So we made courses of action to play, and the primary point she made to me when she got in the vehicle was, "OK, I give. I don't have any idea how to play tennis." We both pretty much passed on snickering — and afterward I beat her in straight sets, or might have beaten her. She fessed up so rapidly that I wasn't irritated. I adored the sincerity and attitude.

There could be no surer method for fizzling than to forfeit who you are for progress, ubiquity or a relationship. Take me, for instance. I was aware as a child that I would never be like Paul Newman or Robert Redford. My nose was broken multiple times and I began going bare at 22. Model material I wasn't. However, I was large, tall, athletic and genuinely savvy. So I turned into that tall person with an extraordinary funny bone. That made me feel at ease, which made other people feel at ease around me. Perhaps you wouldn't go gaga for me from the beginning, however allow me a moment. If you are not careful, I might sneak up on you.

Since then, not much has changed. I appeared in Hollywood, where everybody is under thirty, is tan and has extraordinary hair. Actually take a look at the front of this book on the off chance that you want to revive your memory, yet that isn't what I resemble. A many individuals said, "Gracious, you're fifty, you're going bald and you have that unmistakable Texas drone; that will not work on television." However, I'll let you know right now that in this present reality where everybody is frantically attempting to seem to be Johnny Depp, appearing as though yours genuinely can mean enormous achievement. The way that I'm uncovered alone is sufficient to make me perhaps of the most conspicuous face on television. I am indeed middle-aged. Indeed, I have a one of a kind discourse design. Indeed, I'm not the handsomest fiend to at any point beauty the cinema. Why then? Assuming you're searching for beautiful sight, you have many channels to look over. Just take my for it, no mishap I'm doing a syndicated program, not a look-and-see show. You won't track down me on the WB's new hot-fellow show. I do a television show since talking is my long suit. So on the off chance that you're searching for somebody with a remark, I'm your person.

Think Unique

All in all, individuals who have never gone to considerable lengths to recognize their Personality of You and characterize their item don't respect themselves. It's as if they're still the same vulnerable eighth-grader who was teased because they had a funny shoe or bad haircut. They need to mix in rather than stick out, since, in such a case that they mix in, individuals won't see them to ridicule them or condemn them. The quintessence of the characterized item methodology opposes that kind of rationale since everything revolves around getting taken note.

It's about not accepting a Prada sack in the event that you can't stand to cover the charge card bills. It's about not consenting to go for sushi in the event that you seriously hate crude fish. About not saying you're 29 assuming that you are truly 35. You don't need to be rich. You don't need to adore sushi. You don't need to be youthful. To get along, you don't have to go along. You should simply be authentic. Trust me, there is somebody who might be listening who needs you definitively for what your identity is and what you bring to the table. You simply need to sort out what that is first.

Made in United States
Orlando, FL
18 June 2025

62208937R00066